The Egghead Republic

ARNO SCHMIDT

The Egghead Republic
a Short Novel from the Horse Latitudes

English version by Michael Horovitz
edited by Ernst Krawehl and Marion Boyars

LONDON
MARION BOYARS
BOSTON

First Published in Great Britain in 1979 and the United States in 1980
Reprinted in 1982
by Marion Boyars Publishers
18 Brewer Street, London W1R 4AS
and 99 Main St., Salem, N.H. 03079

First published in Germany in 1957
by Stahlberg Verlag as *Die Gelehrtenrepublik*

© Stahlberg Verlag GmbH, Karlsruhe, 1957
© This translation Marion Boyars Publishers Ltd., 1979, 1982

Australian distribution by Thomas C. Lothian
4-12 Tattersalls Lane, Melbourne, Victoria 3000

Printed by Robert Hartnoll, Bodmin, England

Any paperback edition of this book whether published simultaneously with, or subsequent to, the cased edition is sold subject to the condition that it shall not, by way of trade, be lent, resold, hired out, or otherwise disposed of, without the publisher's consent, in any form of binding or cover other than than in which it was published.

No part of this publication may be reproduced, stored in a retrieval system, or transmitted, in any form or by any means, electronic, mechanical, photocopying, recording or otherwise, except brief extracts for the purposes of review, without the prior written permission of the publisher.

British Library Cataloguing in Publication Data
Schmidt, Arno
 The egghead republic.
 I. Title   II. Krawehl, Ernst   III. Boyars,
 Marion   IV. Die Gelehrtenrepublik. *English*
 833'.912 [F]   PT2638.M453

ISBN 0-7145-2591-X
ISBN 0-7145-2592-8 Pbk

Library of Congress Cataloguing in Publication Data
Schmidt, Arno, 1914-
 [Gelehrtenrepublik English]
 The Egghead republic: a short novel from the Horse latitudes
 / [by] Arno Schmidt; English version [translated from the German] by Michael Horovitz; edited by Ernst Krawehl and Marion Boyars — London; Boston : M. Boyars 1979.

[8] 164 p. ; 21 cm.   GB79-24758
Translation of: Die Gelehrtenrepublik
Includes bibliographical references.

I. Title
PT2638.M453G413   1979   80-670270

833'.914—dc19   AACR 2 MARC

PT2638
.M453
G41S
1979

Foreword to the English edition of *Die Gelehrtenrepublik*

We offer this first English language version of *Die Gelehrtenrepublik (The Egghead Republic)* to the English-speaking world in a spirit of adventure. *Die Gelehrtenrepublik* purports to be a manuscript translated *into* German from a report originally written in American in the years 2008–2009! And if one accepts prophetic fiction as fact (which the reader is invited to do) then what one has here is a *re-translation* not simply into American, but into an American language spoken 30 years hence. To complicate matters even further, Arno Schmidt who is himself a scholar of English, having translated a number of English classics into German, has interspersed his text with phrases in English. Rather than identify these phrases, the publishers have decided to leave it to the literary detective to spot Arno Schmidt's idiosyncratic English interpolations.

Ernst Krawehl, Arno Schmidt's German editor and publisher, meticulously and diligently vetted the first draft of this translation. In addition to the author's linguistic inventions *Die Gelehrtenrepublik* abounds in literary and mythological allusions which require the specialist knowledge provided by Ernst Krawehl. F. Peter Ott, Professor of German at the University of Massachusetts, read the proofs and made many valuable editorial suggestions.

The Publishers

(In accordance with Interworld-Law No. 187, of 4.4.1996, 'Concerning Subversive Documents', where of § 11a takes into consideration the potential publication of politically or otherwise offensive pamphlets by translating them into a dead language, and consolidating the interests of the State as well as those of literature, this manuscript, having been granted Interworld=Licence No. 46, has been translated from Charles Henry Winer's American into German.)

Data

Status as at 1.1.2009	Author	Translator
Age	30.8	67.3
Height (m)	1.84	1.60.5
Weight (pounds)	175	175
State of Health	+ 3.0	− 1.6
Erotic Drive	8.1	0.04
Temperament	sanguine	melancholic — choleric
Profession	Reporter	Director of Studies (emeritus)
Annual Income 2008 (Dollars/Gold)	45.000	2484.37
Vocabulary: American	8.600	3.200
German	1.400	8.580 (of which 3.000 Middle High German)

ORIGINAL TRANSLATOR'S FOREWORD

If the Commission has deemed this document as being worthy of registration and preservation in print, this will in all probability be due above all else to its content, which will in this fashion one day — I hardly dare say it — become 'accessible'. Ever since Audubon published his 'Hints on Hominids' in 1982 (I scarcely need remind the connoisseur just *how* circumspectly expressed *that* was. And in those days there was no restricting Interworld=Law yet in existence: he could have reported quite differently.) We live in virtually total ignorance of the biological developments in a Europe devastated by radioactivity on the one hand, and the American corridor on the other. Thus every contribution is valuable; especially as a considerable stabilization does in fact appear to have occurred in regard to Hexapody.

As far as the actual 'Egghead Republic' is concerned, for every unbiased reader the impression will probably have been created from the second half of the description that follows, that here, too, we have been only very selectively informed — be it by radio or by TV. What they have been trying for all of 30 years to present to us as a 'Floating Parnassus', a 'Helicon in the Sargasso Sea', has now raised doubts in many minds; especially since the, in certain places, embarrassing Open Letter from the Algerian Nobel Peace Prize winner, Abdl el Fadl. Now further data are made available herewith, albeit in a tendentious way and a frivolous tone.—

I submit a personal problem that should not be under-estimated: the translation was from the American into a *dead* language. Since the all-too-prompt atomic annihilation of the Motherland, German as a language has not been able to keep any sort of vital pace with technical or social developments — certain tools, machinery, methods, and also intentions and trains of thought could, consequently, only be rendered by means of circumlo-cution. Quite apart from the very candid and, to say the least, unnecessarily detailed expositions of the author's 'sexual intercourse' — German has fortunately not been able to develop any further terms in this field; none, anyhow, that would be both colloquial and at the same time audacious enough to convey processes such as, for instance, 'Urtication' with all its implications. — When the occasions arise, footnotes will be provided to attempt to fill out gaps of this nature.

As far as the ever recurring pet aversion of the author — who is, after all, of German origin — against all things German is concerned, as well as his, to put it mildly, eccentric mentality, I can only give my assurance that I have taken great pains to supply an accurate translation even of those passages. —

The original of the present text of the 'Egghead Republic' is to be found in the Manuscript Department of the Municipal Library of Douglas/Kalamazoo; the 8 microfilms that were produced from it are located in the places internationally assigned for this purpose. The German translation was made from Specimen No. 5 (Valparaiso).

Chubut, Argentine, 24 December 2008
Chr. M. Stadion

22.6.2008: On cankerstilts of light the straitlaced sunbelly hovering over the landscape.

Late afternoon in the car[1]: checking around again — ? — Yeah: notebook, telescope, green specs; passports and ID. / And the road rattled: sun & cactus blended. My mess of fingers lazed in front of me. The captain smoked alongside (and sang; always on the 'oon' tune: moon and noon and June and racoon — perhaps there are new tribes whose vocabulary is toned down to certain vowel formations?).

"Bad road!" — *But he* shrugged one shoulder: Hm — getting close to the wall. / We'd left Prescott, Arizona, at 1600 hours, and sat in the heat as in amber; (People in synthetic resin blocks: that's been going on for years. To pass on fashions and the like to posterity. No. 238 in the Detroit Museum was my great love once, when I was a boy (tho today it's all, of course, ridiculously old-fashioned; I used to save all my youthful erections for her. Not seen her in eleven years now: the reverie cantered away.)).

That strip of dust on the horizon?: "Yes. It's the wall." (And slowed down; the engine even quieter. We drove straight towards it.)

Then turning Northward; staying in line with it: "No no: 24 feet high!" / And that's no joke, come to think of it: twice 4,000 miles of concrete wall to shut off our American atomic corridor from both sides! (I'm dying to know what things will look like inside the zone: they say troupes of centaurs were spotted in Nevada! Quite apart from other wild rumours. But then I was the first to have gotten a travel permit in eleven years!).

And on and on and on along the endless pale-grey wall of concrete (laid out in 6 × 6 foot blocks). / In back the two bekhakied

---

[1] Almost noiseless, nuclear-driven; I chose the closest of the obsolete concepts.

louts sprawled their total of 13 feet over the mail bags. Now and then the one on the left cigaretted himself: at one point one of them stuck the radio into his ear and heard something funny (facial expressions often reveal what's being lapped up!). / "Do you know the diameter of the wall? How thick and all that?". — He took the bend with care, then shaped his mouth into a pout of indifference; shook his head and spread his shoulder-tips: "What for?" / (Li'll information here).

17.20 hours: "The sentry box." (Finally!). / We effected an elegant quarter-turn and stopped: heads of the garrison showed up instanter on the white walls, in the black openings. / (Thermometer on the door: 35° in the shade. And they forecast warmer weather; charming!).

"Winer? — : How come?!": and I had to present my papers immediately: identity card with photo, thumbprint, tooth structure, penis type. Then the permit, stamped in octuplicate (by every world power) — my carte-blanche to crack the Egghead Republic: nothing like this had happened to them before! / Plus the guillotined sheet certifying the USA's permission to cross the Hominid Zone. (Picked this up several times, the colonel did, lurkingly wrinkled his brow. His thoughts ticked over behind the barricades of his West Point cranium. He betook himself to a rear office with my precious document. Spoke long-distance; volumes. — Reappeared with a smile somewhere in the sticks of his disagreeable military mug: had evidently gone on the nod back there.) And continued nodding:

"Right. — : Well. — : Of course you have to be screened first. And I'm sending an official along; we've got an East wind; that's good." —

In a white courtyard (and my one piece of luggage pathetically = tiny by my side). Across the way a sergeant was trying out my pocket telescope for the regulation 20-fold enlargement maximum (civilians are forbidden any bigger; according to

Interworld so&so: might muck about with the moon, eh?). But the plastic lenses showed exactly 19.74; could've told him that all along; tested by Caltech. And reluctantly he handed it back to me. / Then the doctor was ready:

"Lift up please!": So up I lifted; and the geigercounter's ticktock went sliding on all over me, round me, within me. Over the way, my quite unnecessarily copious blood sample was being sentry-fugued: a spry female assistant cocking her left eye to the microscope (while the right one sized up my naked figure like a wallpaper pattern); her mouth emitted series of numbers. /:"Where d'ya get that crazy hormone count? — Quarrelled with your girlfriend? Huh." (If the truth be known, following the fatherly advice of my friend — the one who'd been allowed to visit the Egghead Republic 8 years ago! — I'd purposely saved 4 weeks' groove-juice. He'd hinted plainly enough (to the wise a word is sufficient) at high jinks on the Turbo-island; that secretaries were hand-picked, in order to make the best possible impression on the reporter, and were put at your disposal for 'dictation'; and I, though only 30, had to make the appropriate preparations.) / "No kidding?: One-hundred-and-forty-three?! — Better check it over again." So over she checked:?: the same count! (And now the WAC risked both her mascara'd eyes!).

All manner of injections: a white one; another white. / "A pale green one?": "OhwellOk! 'case you should get bitten by a=a a—a— spider or something!" He gave an embarrassed grunt. (And secretive=angry additional mumbling: ". . . something quite new . . . against the thingummies(?) . . . : Then that won't be quite so . . ."). —

"Major Bancroft : Mister Winer." / But this one was definitely a nice guy, the 'official' assigned to me! About my age; small and wiry; we looked at each other, several times nodding contentedly. / Even helped me to change. (All the gear I'd brought with me — those few things! — were meticulously

disinfected, then shot by postal rocket across the Zone to Eureka). At this point I was given only a rough-fibred jacket and shorts. A broadbrimmed straw hat up top; sandals of rawhide for my feet. Plus spearstick, compass, sunglasses (my field glasses had been 'accidentally on purpose' sent off by now with the rest of my luggage). The brimful water bottle; 3 days' condensed iron rations into the kit-bag. / "So we're going to fly off together by balloon: yes, it's a pretty old-fashioned life we lead in these parts!"; laughed like a big baby; and we were ever more in sympathy.

"*Well*=*er — another thing Mister Winer:* you're flying off into the Zone on tonight's Easterly wind. As far in as you can get. The rest of the crossing you have to make on foot — Major Bancroft can explain this to you later. — *I* — " (and this 'I' with thoughtful=ponderous emphasis)" — *I* should keep as close as possible to the shade of the big cactus thickets during your march: 'cause it's much . . . cooler there — : er=one moment!!" (for Bancroft's wondering hand craved permission to speak — but he dropped it again in puzzled deference to the hypocritical mask which slipped over the colonel's sufficiently unlovable face! Poor WACs.) / "Oh=just a tick, — you'll excuse us, Mister Winer." (Took my major to one side, right over to the other end of the room; gave orders, emphatically; opened out a finger-fan with at least 5 reasons into the startled babyface; then crunched his hand into a fist (at which point his incisors clenched!) — the Major held his throat with his left, and stroked it: 4 fingertips on one side, 1 thumb on the other. / Finally shrugged his shoulders and click-heeled to attention: he had understood.).

"*Hold on — I'll give you a message to take.*"*;* and right jovially the Colonel held out the little finger's length of black-sealed cylinder: "As soon as you meet someone, pass it on, say you want to see *Pluvus!*". (And vanished, before I could ask, in the first place, who *was* this someone I was supposed to be meeting? And then, who was this famed 'Pluvus'? (Not the most beautiful of names; I wouldn't want to be called that)). / "Do you know?"; but Bancroft had got more buttoned up the while, only shrugged, and chatted on and over and out.

Sundown 19 hours 30?: "No; we have to go on waiting; has to get darker yet. To avoid any disturbance." — I sagely omitted all questions such as *who* might be disturbed. We besat ourselves on the stone bench outside the control-tower, and watched the men playing baseball (a spade stood bang in front of the sundisc; lifted his bat again and again, and hit out as if to smash everything to smithereens:!).

Barrack-room chat: "*About how many* sentry boxes are there?": "One every 30 miles." / Garrison?: "The small ones, like us, 50 men." / "What's the shape of the wall, actually?" — He then drew its cross-section into the sand for me with the swagger-stick: 3 feet thick at the base (and that, by the way, is also the depth of the foundation); 24′ high vertically, on the outside; 9′ wide on the top: "So that you can travel on it by scooter like on a road; if you're in a hurry." — So it's 24′ high inside as well, but slightly overhanging?: "Yes." — And duraluminium struts as supports. :"Yes."

The sun sank: the line of mist around its arc turned bloody; cartloads of yellow piled high. (Soon it would be green; then colder still. Gusts of Easterly wind came over the Nevada desert, shivering our shoulder timbers.) / But we had to wait. (And these sandals really took some getting used to. Though everybody wore them here).

Barrack-room chat No.2 then: "Oh, you too were in the European war?!"; he poked his animated face in my direction, and warmed up even more. It turned out that in 1990, when we were twelve, we'd not only been in the same battle-sector, but in the same regiment even, though he was with the underwater battalion in the Caspian Sea (which was reduced to atomic spray following a forecast of South Wind, and dispersed across Western Russia: he described that very vividly: how they'd camped for weeks in this plastic bell at the bottom of the sea: the shoals of giant sturgeon: fights with underwater Russians. How they, 20 seconds 'before', flew off over the neutral Arab block (and escaped being shot down by them by 1 hair's breadth!). And he got quite excited going over that again!). / Though I'd been only a humble coding clerk, I still knew all the names and details. We shook hands repeatedly, laughed; and nodded ardently. (He certainly seemed hot and bothered — and especially when we were most in accord — : why?!)

The time-honoured mobilization of the stars. And 1 Lance=corporal, saluting:! / At the ready again. / Major Bancroft rose with a sigh; strangely undecided. And we went in single file to the patio, where our balloon was being filled: funny prospect, floating along in such an old-fashioned orb! (21 feet diameter; load capacity 215 kilograms: we were weighed in full kit —, —, — : found too light. Bancroft, mumbling, got himself another little bag of something: still not enough! Well, another round hundredweight of sand on board:? — right; that's it! / We lay on our bellies in the flat-based wicker basket of the gondola. Side by side. 6 couldn't-care-less privates held the ropes. Once again I courteously bowed (lying down; must have looked cute!) toward the Colonel's illuminated mug; which shone peculiarly bent in the night (or was it we who were hanging bent?), and rasped military politesse. "Uh=you're welcome. — Take care, Bancroft!". / Whereupon the 6 faces suddenly got much smaller! My shocked stomach contracted — — :! —

Nothing at first (eyes craved time to attune to the darkness). But I could hear Bancroft murmuring confidently at my side; he had the illuminated compass-dial under his nose; after that, the watch — and things must somehow have 'tallied'; for he croaked contentedly. / "Well-now: we can relax for the first 6 hours: the sun rises at 4.30. And the wind still getting stronger: so we'll make our 3 to 400 miles — if we're pushed I can groove on up a li'l bit higher." / "Naw: we'll never ever get *all* the way across the Zone; we'd need a fullblown Easterly *gale* for that! — And you can't fly by day: mustn't do anything to upset the Centies unnecessarily." Which brought us straight to the nub!:

"The Centies?" — : "Yeahyeah, the Centaurs." — Then immediately went cautious again: "You better store up on your sleep; strenuous days are ahead," he evaded (probably wanted to think something over, wanted, as it were, 'to be alone'.) / So I politely crossed my arms, laid my forehead to rest on them; and tried to doze; (at least for a while, till moon-rise in ninety minutes; else I wouldn't see a flying=sausage). He continued to breathe, aloud, ill at ease.

But must have dropped off; for when he nudged me and muttered "fasten your belt", everything underneath lay dipped in sleepy-yellow light, and the two-thirds moon lingered to our left, facing us. We lay at an angle — feet lightly raised, head inclined downwards; and while I slipped my arm into the sling he explained: having established from the behaviour of a couple of weeny nightclouds that a sharp airstream was steaming up Westward, he'd, released a little sand; and had merrily floated into it. Now we were really getting 'a decent bite' (as witness the rattling of the ropes and an occasional flispering of the silken globe around and above us).

On the right a couple of wrecked constellations: "*Is it still* really radioactive down there?": "H'm; not noticeably. — For the most part even less than on the rest of the earth; 'course, there are no reactors in the Zone; no generators, no machines, nix: so there's no fallout at all . . ." and he slumped his shoulders forward.

"How clearly one sees the 'Red Patch'!" — He gyrated his head, grunted something about "considerable libration"; and gazed across at the moon with me for quite a time. (Both the USA and the USSR were supposed to have shot their entire load of

'fissile materials' — exactly 2,000 missiles each — into the Wargentian Crater in the South, and the result had been a right ballyhoo in that plain, as was visible even at the time of the New Moon. Well, now it was 'under control', as they assured us at each and every fart (from which any child could see with its arse closed, that the test explosions had only been transferred into interplanetary space: why else the diverse unnaturally bright shooting=stars?! (And most of them couldn't, of course, be seen; because they happened beyond the flip-side of the moon.))).

"I was up there once," he ruminated, "—when I was a courier." :???

"Noway!: You don't notice the trip at all: you're put to sleep — and suddenly you're there!" / But get this: he'd seen maps which gave 'spheres of interest' and 'lines of demarcation': the Russians sat on the Northern rim of Serenitatis; the Yanks had their bases in Bianchini, on the Sea of Rainbows.[2] The Chinese were cautiously poised between the cliffs of Picard, smack in the dustbowl of the Mare Crisium. / "No: you don't *see* a thing! You're stuck, like in a glass bottle: a terrible let-up, the whole thing."

While he was still talking, the hair on the back of his head went blonder; more yellow. And he too threw a grumpy backward half-look; puffed up his cheeks uneasily: "The sun goes up in 50 minutes. Have to start down."

Slowly down to berth: in his hand he held the lead to the valve (from which, at the North Pole of our balloon, a gaseous hissing emerged). We lay there like the snakes of old, his face restlessly scanning the straight-upside-down terrain: stretches of sand; plant islands; "That dark green lot are cactus-thickets"; ("Ah: that's where I'm to keep my heels cool" I interpolated heedfully): he didn't take his peepers off the

---

[2] Sinus Iridum, according to current nomenclature.

bird's eye view; and furthermore opened his mouth, in order to sharpen his look-out . . . . .)

Then all of a sudden his handonarm reached out and up:!: The roar increased at once; and we pushed down so fast it was almost unbearable:! (But these boys had experience: he let it snap shut with such dexterity that we came to a standstill at about 20 yards above the sand — down here the air was practically still — ; then a last delicate tug — : — and our wickershell sat itself down imperceptibly).

"*No: keep lying down!*" (right: first he had to let some more gas out; had I stood up, the whole caboodle — and he with it — would have gone straight up in the air again!).

"*Well now: let's take hold of the sandbag together* please — Heave-ho!" — :

And before we could say boo the lightened balloon-skin shot like an eagle into the blue! (And after ten seconds could only be recognized as a tiny disc; if you hadn't followed its direction you couldn't have seen it at all. He nodded satisfaction: another mission accomplished as per HQ!). / Next, empty the sandbag; bury the shell: . . ; : . . . .

"*Now, here's your gear* —" (his glance came to light on the compass they'd given me for the march — and stiffened: "What's that?":?)

Several times over he compared it to his own: and once again, *this* way round:? Hands on hips; and thought; mumbled something ending in "balls-up". / "The poles of your compass are reversed, see!: The needle points South instead of North! — What the . . ."

And suddenly got very energetic: "Let's have your calabash!". So I handed over my yellow-green half-gallon gourd. He pulled out the stopper; sniffed:,,,,,?: poured a drop into his palm and sampled it with the tip of his tongue: "Man, this sure is — :

Gin!". "Oh; that's dandy!" says I, delighted; but his profile flashed black: "You'd be surprised: in this heat!" Food for thought. "That damned cookhouse orderly!!". (Took the folded map from one of his breast-pockets, examined and compared).

(Dead straight horizon: the watery yellow, enormously squashed expanse of the sun. / 5 minutes later: its contours frayed like sun-flowers! A storm?).

"*Here, take mine as well;* it's water." (Slung it round me without asking. And I let him do it; I had a feeling he meant the best for me). / "My compass too: I'll make do with my wrist-watch meanwhile." / "The spear's supposed to have a crosspiece: have mine. — And this electrostick as well: you just press the button and gently connect with the tip; that's enough to throw the toughest Centy, beard an' all!" So I fastened that, too, on to my wide leather bandolier.

Ingenuous broad grin in his direction: "Thanks a lot, Major!" — He nodded goodbye, his lower jaw grimly tightened (had to make it North-East; on some 'tour of inspection'. I had a good 35 miles ahead of me; always West-North-Westward: "Bye=bye!").

Well then, a heave at the matchbag; and turn my back on that loathsome sun! — Wasn't exactly easy walking on sand; but things ought to improve in the evening.

"*Um = hello! — Mister Winer?!*" — : What now? Back again? (And his face very severe; the honest profile almost turned away; he spoke with deliberate care):

"*I!*" (and how emphatic this "I"!): "*I: never* walk through cactus fields!". / Let his eloquently pointed right slowly sink. Tetchily drew his head between incommunicado shoulders. Stumped off (his back told me that I wasn't allowed any more questions). — . — .

Stood drawing figures in the sand with the spear-cum-walking-stick. Then a shake of the head, and march off at the double: weird folks, the military: never see through 'em. (Everyone always keeping some crap or other 'secret'; I know how it is myself.)

But extremely decent to leave me alone like this, in the Zone, without supervision or indoctrination: so one's free to form a subjective-objective opinion. (And if one knows the 'personal equation' this becomes even purely objective: because those philologists had gradually learnt how to subtract the individuality of a writer from the text.)[3] / And the feet below strode nimbly over yellow and brown.

Interesting flora! (Although, of course, I wasn't trained enough to identify which were classical species and which might be recent mutations. Not really my province at all; one has one's work cut out to be something of an expert in 1 subject. Unlike my great-great-uncle, the notorious polymath — must've been quite a character!)

These here tut-tuts, for instance!: Dark brown square-cut hollow rods sticking straight out of the sand. Thorns the length of my little finger. No leaves to make up for them. And always these 5-petalled flowers alternating with lemon-like fruits: are they edible? (Better not try; might taste of gall. Or worse still, of nothing at all; so the imagination runs riot, into diarrhea. Plus vomiting: no fear!)[4]

Stand on a tiny mound of sand and look around:?: Behind, the sun, with its still unlovely complexion (just like the Colonel last night). / A circular horizon, cut and polished. / Far ahead on the right a cluster of giant cacti: their candelabranches a good 60 feet high! — More to the left, more in my direction, another flat parcel of mist: must be one of those empty gallery forests they'd muttered about. / Well, up and at 'em!

---

[3] Particularly recommended to all readers in the case of this author.
[4] The description would indicate *Acanthosicyos horrida*. Unless it is really a new species.

Walking; again and again, shaking my head in thought: what the last two wars had led to! / Europe laid waste, atomized. Here the great Zone. / Pope removed to Nueva Roma. (Near Bahia Blanca; where they'd immediately built a new St. Peter's: all the relics were saved, it seems). / Jerusalem gone (an Egyptian, so it was said . . . Whereupon an Israeli of course instantly zoomed off on a pilgrimage to Mecca: Hadji!) / And marching on hale and hearty the while.

On the edge of the dustwood: I liked it! Nice and empty and desolate: quiet. / Once more I took my direction from the sun and entered, walking between the solitary trunks.

Inside the dustwood: the finest sandclocksand underfoot. (Here and there a largish corn-yellow patch of flattened dry grass: straw blades with their very sharp edges!). / Every 30 yards a slender little pale-barked trunk (but darkly panthered at regular intervals; the bark). Its stiff umbrella crown 9 feet from the ground. Once in a way they stand closer together, only 3 paces apart. / No undergrowth whatever: très sympathique! At one point, a screaming red mushroom (or more precisely: a thing with a cap: when you peeped underneath, or looked at the coiled stalk — hm hm hm.)

I cast no shadow; nothing did: like a grey flat sea filled with seaweed and algae (but then what was I meant to be?). / A thicket loomed from afar; I slipped the loop of my electrostick onto my wrist; much better.

Or am I going to perish?! — So I stopped still, under the leafpatterned sky. / And suddenly everything fell into place with new comprehension: 93° proof gin instead of water. Reversed compass. Plus that frequent insidious pointer towards the lovely shaded cactus groves?! / But Bancroft had been decent: *and* crafty!: If they were now to interrogate him under hypnosis (as we're wont to do in these days for any old tripe): he'd never *expressly warned me* not ever to go in, like "Don't go in there under any circumstances." No; he'd merely stated: "*I never* go through cactus fields!" / Well, that's put me in the picture at last!

Striding on more quickly; pointing my head gingerly = faster this way and that. (And back, maybe:? — : no; all quiet still. The grey wigs of the trees above).

So there was something in there all along!!: Enough to finish you off, man! / Better get the lance off my hump: could it be 'Centies', perhaps? Might be fabulous creatures! / Can I make 35 miles in a day?: what with that sand not bloody lik...

and stared at each other! My mouth gaped open; left thumb pressed the button, cleverer than me, my right guided the spear's blade...

:"Oh= no" she said sleepily (I'd never heard anyone speak so slowly!). And went on chewing at her spikes of grass. — : why should a naked girl be lying here? And bestride a (dead?) deer?!

She pulled a fresh stalk from the coarse-fibred pouch by her side; eyed it critically; took a trial nibble. — Then (in the self-same slow-motion intonation: some consonants extraordinarily heavily accented, and a mighty powerful voice withal; droll): "You're no forester".[5] she decided. A couple more bites. Raised her body: — !

Dead deer and all !!!: My hand flew to my forehead (and my fingers stared at her, flabbergasted; to say nothing of my mouth): so this. : was a centauress?? — —

So this was a centauress!: she let me walk round her, several times while she watched me, serenely amused and resigned. — :

A fabulous ashblonde stand-up mane, which started above her forehead in an impudent forelock, amenable to fringe or back-

---

[5] In the original version the word 'ranger' is used; it will become apparent later why I have at times used the designation 'forester'.

swept styling: channelled down a sweet nape of neck, and on between the shoulderblades; continued at hand-height along the backbone; till it finally tumbled over into her black-tasselled tail.

Rather like a Grant-gazelle from the rear: quite a tautly stretched close-cropped pelt; back and outer shanks of pale russet hue. Belly and inside legs white: 4 slim legs.

And up front — a naked girl, no less; with arms! — Now I stood facing her, and she inclined her narrow high head, and laughed at me : ? / The nose: its wide bridge firmly joined to her forehead. A long red mouth. Throat. Ivory shoulders, smooth and sleek. Teenage bubs. Slender hips. Long girls' legs (and hooves to boot: almost as if a modern, hard lady's shoe had taken root at the ankle).

Back to the face (stop: large, pointed, brown velvet ears yet; windwardly, flappable). (About 5'5 tall[6]: that figures). She smiled patiently; archly. And her tongue ran one lap round her lips: it was considerably larger than mine; hence presumably the thicker diction!).

"What's your name?" came to me. : "Thalia"[7] her face said; persistently, "You're no forester." / No; I was not. But I stood still, as if bewitched. (Which I was, without a doubt!: Her tail flicked at her side, one lash).

Bewitched: "Gee, are you *pretty!*" — And I really meant it true. (And got an erection from savouring her pearlike breasts, as was apparent in my baggy trousers; she blushed with childish pleasure.) / We were soon trying out each other's names! No sooner had she coquettishly moved away than — : "Thalia!" — and she swept round on her hind legs, and executed the most exquisite courvette; so close that her nipples were almost

---

[6] Equals 1.65 meters by the old German measure.
[7] American pronunciation; something like "Ssáldscha" transcribed into German, with pretty sharply lisped "Ss" at the beginning. — Likewise her subsequent "Tschaa-Lieh".

touching mine. (Then I had, perforce, to play my part and haughtily withdraw; whereupon she at once uttered, "Charley" — and when I turned back she was standing there expectantly, virginally coy, holding the tuft of tail in her left hand.)

"Coming along for a bit?". (And I asked with every intention, and fully aware of the deed to be done: I'd be much safer in her company — at least in regard to all centaurs! Besides, her conversation might yield vital information about the dangers of the Hominid-Zone.

She nodded ardently and long: "Oh; gladly." She was ready to give way at the fore-knees and dip her ashblonde crest grasswards: which I gallantly forestalled, handing up her gear: a spear like mine. A leather-bandolier (drinking-flask and provender bag attached), which she sported from one shoulder to the other hip. And a sunhat yet, with broad, floppy brim (which, hey ho, she stuck on the back of her head; old Florentine style — : "Neat!"). —

Side by side: our 6 feet rustled in the sappy sand. Very quiet. The half-tones of our chat. Serene foliage above. (As high as our spearpoints could reach). / Once we came upon a wide clearing dotted with mimosa-shrubs: when we looked round, standing once again under a pair of spindly trees, we could retrace our path exactly from the uninterrupted wake of droopy drowsy foliage. (And exchange smiles at that. — As if by accident, I laid my hand on that place where girl and gazelle met — my fingers probed deliciously deep into the resilient upright mane : ! — and she kept still).

How to make conversation with a young centauress? — Best simply get going, eh? / "How old are you?". — "Oh". she said, "it's my birthday today: all of 24 Gow-chromms." — " 'Gow-chromms'?"; first she had to describe what she meant: what shines crooked by night, ever changing round. (Definitely the moon!). / And further explanation: at 20 moons of age they get their outfit (she dabbed at her food-bag) including weapons. At 40 they have to become mothers. / Drinking water? : all rivers ended up in salt-marshes; a few hot springs were known.

The cactus fields?! : She immediately frowned and bared her strong teeth scornfully: "Never=nevers hang out in there!" / Pell-mell, my imagination leapt into action: huge praying mantises, greenskinned articulated beasts? — She saw from my hands that I had absolutely no idea; and let me in on what the pig of a colonel had mapped out for me:

Never=nevers! : *The mutational jump* had been directed — by means of excessive radiation — towards hexapody, generally speaking.[8] In other words: manifold combinations of various types of human forms on the one hand, and insects and hooved beasts on the other, had evolved. Out of all the ephemeral confusion, these centaurs seem to have presented themselves as tolerably stable. Alongside the abovementioned Never=nevers. (And, furthermore, a third type, of which I couldn't form a reasonable conception from her muddled description; seemed relatively harmless though. If I was not mistaken, this also had a human face?).

Anyhow, the Never=nevers: these were giant spiders! The soft, poison-grey belly about half a yard in diameter. A human head up front (with all manner of new button-features: the ears had been discarded, for instance, in favour of dot-eyes); plus proboscis. Poison-claws on two frontal feet; so heavily loaded that two sufficed to knock the toughest centaur unconscious. Four were lethal!

Hence the 'spider-spear' with the crossbeam; and she demonstrated: the monster was impaled on it; thrust into the sand; and finally bludgeoned to death. / But they never voluntarily left their cactus-thickets, moist shadows. Where they spun their webs, out of virtually unbreakable wire-thick

---

[8] Six-footedness.

threads. And so trapped foolhardy young centies (and also the elderly and ill, or those stupefied by poisoned grasses). — Alternatively that 'third type' which, I understood by degrees, came in 2 variants. / Anyway, deadly enmity was established. (And I, too, shuddered thinking to myself: how trustingly I was going to seek out those cooling shades. Might well have risked a nap hard by the foot of one of those hairy pillars — : what a dirty dog, that commander!! / And indeed the entire military police: didn't want an inkling to leak out, huh; in fact, only granted my permit with the insidious provision that I should certainly never come back.

(Well, I'd have to be veryvery careful — now and whenever! A prohibition to publish would be the very least. Should I manage to get through alive. (And to this end, had to start by getting off well with my fair Thalia; going the whole hog!)).

"Thalia?!" : She pushed her lower jaw forward, and emitted a deep hedonistic "Mmmm?". I placed myself in front of her. Grasped her 2 smooth shoulders; (these she withheld only slightly; so that her bosom thrust farther forward: artful!). She raised the outer extremes of her elongated eyebrows diagonally. Began panting more and more urgently. Her white flank pressed closer sideways, hoof to shoulder. The tail whipped agitatedly rightleftright: Leftrightleft. / (And then our first dexterous kiss!)

She probed my rugged coatskin with wild unpractised fingers:? — so I threw it off. And made so bold as to take a breast in each mitt: (tremendously firm; like white-leather pears. The whole frontal third a pouting raw-rosy point). / She couldn't hold out any longer. Wheezed sweetly from the throat; flung her sinewy arms over my shoulders, and squeezed our breasts together. Eyes closed. Stuck a huge portion of tongue in my mouth (and tasted good and warm; of grass-seeds; I thought of spelt and aristae, grain-mouth, threshers . . . ? — :.' — :

perhaps a fine high-pitched barking under the ground?! — But she didn't relax our embrace; only cocked her large ears once, vigilantly (till it occurred to me too, that it was only prairie-dogs. And right lustily I hove to once more).). —

Hurry to a more intimate spot (yet was I pestered by countless major scruples!). / But the shadow of her lemony hatbrim bobbed so cutely over her cheek. And she held my hand so diligently. And confessed:

"*Shilbit — my girlfriend* — she went with a forester for 14 days. And told me *everything:* ohhhhh!". She snorted and threw her chest back in raptures: "Can you do that? It's permitted for us, at 20: the *lot!*"

In the thicket then (and she stood ready; her first time; bubbling with joy). / So I did my level best (and a damn comical situation it was, too: had to keep my eyes closed all the time! Except when she tilted her face back at the most dangerous angle: it didn't quite reach, but at least we kissed the air in front of our faces. And like that one could imagine a girl.) / Till I began to get paralysed. On account of the clicking French style.[9])

Breathing, panting from our labour of love; her flanks all a-tremble; side by side we lay. / Her forelegs buckled. All her warm places. The blond tail still rocketed above us now and then: Both of us. Her raised head started to nod; she murmured: "That tasted good, back there!" (Fervent nodding; the breastbuds nodded too; each time I caught one; with my lips; at which she slumbrously laughed. And at last laid the yellow bush of her head beside mine. (And lazy kissing. And grassbreath.)).

---

[9] Incomprehensible. — The speech of those centaur-types is a slightly corrupted American — as is irreproachably indicated by the foregoing — and the following. But one will have to get accustomed to such inaccuracies owing to the — possibly dilettante, novitiate haste of the author —.

(How many 'moons' have I got on my back, incidentally? In case she should ask: 30 times 12 ('can't work; so I'll borrow me one'). The balance of my 29.5 cyclic days on top of that; plus another 4 or 5 . . . makes about . . . . what: 375. So I'll say 100. (Or 80?). — In case she asks.) —. —.

Slept a bit without thinking! (But the sun was still high: for a second I thought I'd dreamt *'the lot'*. Till I took several looks at her; she was wide awake by now).

Deep in thought, she bent her head; drew it to her, and munched at the tip. Wound her long muscular tongue round it (so rough, it felt hairy!); pulled it into shape, and swallowed away[10]: that's what they call siesta! . . . .

Walking along again, about this & that: they each had a small pair of nickel pliers in his bag to snip the thorns off the succulents so's they can guzzle the thick-juicy flesh. (While I was looking at the stainless tool, she sauntered aside; discreetly relieving herself of her little droppings; and wiped herself carefully, several times (with many leaves). And came ambling to my side again). / To my question?: Yes. They could vary the pace as they pleased. And did it too, especially on longer excursions, so that they used all their muscles in turn: sometimes trotting, sometimes normal.

"The heat's terrific!" But she only shrugged her shoulders sadly: "If you want to make it to World's End by tomorrow . . .". (So that's what they call the giant wall. Absolutely logical really: no one has seen the other side! — Or have they? Hardly likely.)

Then we lit upon a wide sandy plain. Only every 2 or 3 miles one of these accursed cactus islands: a hundred paces in diameter tall as houses and thorn-thicketed. (And if you cared to imagine the Sleeping Beauties within!) — At regular intervals she reared herself up: then she grew three hands taller than me! — And reconnoitred . . . .:? . . . . .

---

[10] The author means a stem of buffalo-grass, Buchloe dactyliodes Engelm., if I understand him aright.

And suddenly started to tremble; nostrils flaring, but not in fear; the lower jaw pressed forward . . . .: "Quick" she commanded (in a gross growling contralto that suddenly seemed to roll out of her throat-barrel). Then 50 springy leaps towards something; I was left behind (and quick as lightning knelt in the sand?):

A dead little Centaur-calf!!: she hastily ran her hands over it; lifted the limp little legs — and showed me the swollen red punctures: "Never=never!" she neighed. Touched once more:?: "Maybe it's still alive?" Deliberated, her lower jaw grinding angrily, and leapt in the air like a steel spring:

A circus-pirouette on hindlegs, scanning the horizon: the sun was *there,* aha. Here *this* stone; that lone tree there?: "Wait here!" she cried: "Nono, nothing'll happen! — And in ten minutes you stick your hat on the tip of the spear and hold it as high as you can: I'll get the others!" Leant her chest forward, arms crossed over her bosom so that each hand was holding the other shoulder — and made off, ventre à terre, leaving clouds of sand showering round my nose!

: Man, did she work fast!!: in no time at all she was racing ahead between 2 clusters of trees over there; propelled herself into the air on all fours; flew off like a bird over some large obstacle; went storming across the farthest visible hillock — : and vanished. / I sat down on the stone in dismay.

(Or perhaps better stand up!: In case one of those beasts comes spinning along from somewhere!) (But I couldn't fathom that dog, all things considered! : he'd kept rambling on about *his personal predilection* for *shade.* — What a swine!) / Two minutes, at a guess.

And this poor little one!: I tenderpityingly tucked my jacket over him; so he'd at least be in some sort of a shade. / Three minutes.

Or should I try a slug of gin? — I knelt down — stop; another look round? — OK: air & earth seemed 'all clear'. — into the sand next to the pale teeny head; decorked the bottle; then hesitated, solemn. / First take thought: five minutes!: the effect would likely be similar to snakepoisons. (What'ya mean 'likely'? Merely a personal hypothesis!) But let's suppose, then. Like the book always says: 'alcohol in large doses'. / Or maybe they know of special herbs? — But homeopathic herbiage of that ilk is usually much too copious, weak, ineffectual against such strong poison: else no 'natural man' would've died of snakebite in the past: six minutes!

Ok, down with it, what?: So I prized open his jaw; poured a full measure into the hollow stopper; and inspirited him in two instalments — he was only a child, after all. / Seven minutes. (Or was it eight already? Nope, six more like; for I felt slightly eerie; in which state, experience tells, you tend to count more quickly! Specially if you're standing in need of succour. Better say seven again? sobeit: seven!).

Didn't the kid's eyelids begin to flutter?! Or did I see wrong, eight? / No!: His tailpiece, too, hit a short tremolo: lovely!

But now, to be on the safe side, make ready with the signal; the beacon, to take a bearing from: 'Siehst, Vater, Du den Hut dort auf der Stange?''[11](one of the jokes I still knew in the language of my forefathers : bet they never dreamt their scion'd one day make it with a Centauress.) / Yeah, you keep shakin, that tail o'yours! — Now's the time, surely. / (Good job I had my sunglasses; even so, it shimmered in front of my eyes (and itched all over; as when there's talk of fleas — in whatever company — each and everybody discreetly starts to scratch.)[12] (Or lice.) / Or Never=Nevers: something rustling? ! — — : No; the stripling again.

---

[11] From Schiller's *William Tell*.
[12] Characteristic of the 'company' the author is apparently in the habit of keeping; noscitur ex socio.

There! Wasn't it trembling? The ground?! Very faintly? I loosened up all I could, uncramped —; — and felt a definite vibration: so hoist the hat! Over there, where Thalia had disappeared to:! —. —:

And then came a thundering towards me, like a convoy of juggernauts!!: Two hundred centaurs clomping in grooves of cast-iron hooves! / Athletes up front (and on the wings to protect their flank): throwing up a flat gust of dust (from which new ones emerged!) (Dust like the fabled Sitting Bull country, goddamnit!).[13] / I'd waggled about my sombrero with such panache that I pulled it down shame facedly now (was well surrounded by now).

Veins thick as clotheslines in their furore!: Thalia came close alongside a broad-shouldered champ (a big black beard he had, that feller; *and* a ditto horn to top it all, like a giant corkscrew, on his forehead.). He saluted briefly, spear in muscular mitt. And lowered himself next to us into the sand.

"Is he still alive? If only he could tell us where!" — And, to my concerned inquiry: "Oh yes, he's bound to die: he's been jabbed three times; there's no remedy." / At this I resolutely yanked my gin bottle forward once more: it seemed there was nothing to lose. (And it might just help; ergo, once more — in she goes!).

In she goes: alcohol in large doses: certainly, sir! / The leader first called a few to stand guard, to look out, toujours en vedette. Then he looked me over, right curiously; (and Thalia, also, proudly scanned the onlookers:! (And they seemed to be perfectly familiar with humans in the shape of "rangers")).

There!!: it snapped the little bugger's eyes open; to start with he whimpered piteously — his mother instantly pushed herself

---

[13] I assume that this is another example of the wontedly intimate=indecent confessions of the author (interbraccal processes?); anyway in the original it quite indisputably has: 'Sitting Bull'!

to his side; quivering; stroked him and hummed a bass recitative. He munched a morsel from her breast. Wider awake (tho I detected the schnapps in his shining sight sockets: must stir a storm, if they're not in the habit!). / The leader butted in; raised a monitory index finger (at which his horn dipped down in slanting parallel lines: another crazy gadget!)

"There: over there.": the nipper pointed feebly to the wirestiff rotunda of horrorplants: "I only ate a couple of herbs. And then I felt awful. And the light went faint . . ." his little voice dwindled away again; head flopped down on mama's arm (who looked at me alarmed:?. — Well now. — : Guess she has to give him a couple of stoppersfull every half hour; to stimulate the heart. With fantastic batmanic gestures I handed over The Great Flask. With emphatic warnings against abuse:!!. — And turned again towards the rest of 'em.)

Who were jabbering away like mad. (And gazing around, happen to notice most of 'em had that reddish-white pelt. (One really Burgundy-red, though, with massive lyreshape horns; seemed altogether badly constructed (expert judgment, what?))). / All of 'em heavily armoured: spider-spear; bow & arrow. Clubs of every shape and weight classification. The 5-man posse round the leader (making 6 in all) appeared to be the only ones with hefty choppers, hung on their shoulder-straps.

"Thalia?!": already she stood beside me, at the ready for any excited briefing. / No: it had been a long time since Never=Nevers had sallied this far South! Yonder, on the Northern Border, yes; systematic spider-slaughters were held up there and the creatures driven even further back; as much as possible.

"Ok — what next?": Now the leaders would rub up fires; which takes about an hour. Then that cluster of shrubbery would be set alight till the Never=Nevers could stand it no longer,

would have to come out: to be speared; the eggs destroyed. /
Ten hefty males were already setting off at a trot, armed with
scythes: "They're mowing off that grasstongue to the right; so
that the fire can't spread." (Others — children and females —
were busy hauling sand, and shaking it on for good measure.)

But a whole hour, eh?: I *turned* to the head-man. Said brusquely:
"You need fire?: I'll do that in a flash!". Showed him the
matchbox. He nodded in deference, joyfully; and immediately
called the bowmen together. They deftly wrapped balls of
dried grass around their arrow-tips.

"Ready, everybody?" — :

I applied the little flame to the heap of thorns, twigs, leaves and
blades —, —, crackle & pop: at your service! / Each in turn
immediately dunked his wooden stave; took up position in
line, facing the cactus-thicket, and let fly his shot: in a lofty
parabola flew the fuşillade, brightly set ablaze by the moving
air: a good half landed according to plan, behind the dark
green wall.

"Always at ten feet distance: that's the stuff!": we drew round in
formation of a giant circle (from whose centre smoke was
beginning to emanate; and explosive sound as of pistol-shots
when the dessicated Opuntine balloon bodies burst). / "You
never know in advance just where they'll come out." —.—

By now the smoke was pagoda-high! (And the noise hellish: a she-
flame ran and pirouetted up one of the pillar-cacti, poised,
made herself a kimono of smoke (which she opened, at
intervals, cocquettishly: presently the whole front became
pale grey, blurred) . . .

:"Look out!" — —

:"There!!": For it came lumbering out from under the billowy
smoke-hem, flat and fast. A slim one stormed at it full tilt, a

jab! and he was away again, ramming the spear deep into the sand; grabbed a spare one from the hand of an attendant maiden, and came smartly galloping back.

The head-man by my side raised a boxer's arm, reared up (to add the weight of his fall to the ramming impact!) — and it instantly wiggled broad and grey on his lance: he rammed downward with his left: and impaled it in the sand.

"They want to get through here!: This' a'waaaay!!!": Thalia had laid her torso forward horizontally, making one line with the ridge of her back; peered into the smoke-curtains and screamed hoarsely: "Heeeeeahh!!" / — :!:!!:

She speared one; trampled on another: one was clinging to her foreleg and was about to dig its claws in, but I tore it off with my bare hands — though it gave me the creeps — and rammed my spear through the pulpy brute! — I picked up the stiff I'd been sitting on, lifted it high over my head and thrust my arms down with all my might upon the next one: making the juice squirt! / Even now four more knights appeared to right and left with lances, wheeling quick as lightning: and there on each spearhead it hung, like a fat mushy pillow — ugly moronsters! —

"Quiet!! — Everybody back to his post: 'case there are more to come!": the leader, with a sheaf of spears in each hand. He gave me and Thalia two apiece. And backed into his place again.

Waiting: the smoke was being sucked by its own fire. Above the conflagration rose the heated air; down below, from all sides, cold streams converged: visibility was reestablished. / And the cactuswood had practically disappeared!: A few exceptionally thick stumps were still glowing; but these also dissolved into smoke and ash before our very eyes. Through and over it, we could already see the cordon on the other side.

"Yeah. — It's over and done with", opined the matter-of-fact leading basso on my right. / And I was scared out of my wits, he was bawling so (do these guys have lungs! WOW.): "Over here, all of you: bring 'em along!"

The victims: sixteen net, no less! Most of them still alive on the pale of their lances and wriggling furiously; flailing about them; you had to watch out not to be thumped by them, even now!

Here; this one; copped it! So it's grey. And fat. And covered with a thin horny flexible skin. Scorpiomen. A fatally European face stuck out in front: small eyes; long hairy feelers hanging down vertically; the whole tailor-made for a night-fury's career. The mouth snoutily poised, ideal for the death-suck. The poison-claws on the frontal stilts, finger-long and curved like a buzzard's beak: revolting!

And still I turned round nervously towards that noise:?: the little centaur calves, male as well as female, had been gathering the squishy egg-sacs; I walked over and had a look: 6 to 8 eggs each; white the size of ping-pong balls: they placed them on a stone and crushed the things with their hooves — like pistolcaps, bang here; there: bang! (And enjoyed themselves and laughed. There they go; on the one hand, I could see how they felt).

But really: such brutes! I gave unfeigned expression to my disgust — and got happy nods all round. / The extinguished fire gave off its sharp aroma where smoke rippled on. (The rest were cut up with spades, and the pieces buried). / "We've had 190 at a time before now!" / But finding them hereabouts only happens — oh — once every ten Gowchromms." (Still: once a year!). / We disposed ourselves slowly towards the tribal grazing-grounds and talked: about them, about me, about them. (Thalia always at my side. At one point an enormously tall greeneyed demi-virgin manoeuvred herself near — "my girlfriend"; but then she'd made shiny=big eyes at me; and dumbly edged closer & closer, —; till Thalia, full of indignation, chased her away!).

"Oh, you have an hour or 2 to spare: The end of the world is nigh." : "Well, for people like you!" (This answer pleased him visibly; he stroked his massive block of beard and effected a proud forward leap).

Names like earthquake! : one patch of ground we came across was called 'Tatarakáll' (and the hollow drumming sound of hooves was the same!). —

In — well, could you call it the 'village'?: the few leafy huts made of broken-off branches (a few of them munched quite bare by the very hungry or very lazy ones!). / Everybody was once more engaged in completely peaceful business: bearded centaurs stood in the meadows wielding their scythes. (One, all silhouette, raised his bottle, drinking; (I pinched myself in the leg: had I fallen asleep over a Greek mythology primer?)).

No! : Never & No-how! : A centauress with spectacles was something new for sure (and elderly too: an iron bucket dragging on her arm: they liked to hold their ampler breasts with both hands while galloping, the older ones. — A bra factory. Could make a fortune!).

And all these names, like Thunderstorm, like Slingshanks, like Fiery Air; like Bare Earth, Heated Crucible, Chiselled Gold[14] (and the head-man had a tool! like the flute-tootling pied piper of Hamelin; what chance had a puny ranger!).[15]

There: a zebroid-girl! : a black stripe parted her narrow impudent face down the middle, from her forehead down to the base of her throat; (but then it slanted right, one white

---

[14] I don't know what the author is trying to hint at here; perhaps it is meant to be poetry. Anyway I am translating the syllables literally.
[15] Flautists must appear perfectly bucolic — appropriate to any thinking man. Admittedly, the simple classic little instrument might have appeared primitive to the 'foresters'.

the other black as coal: boy, did that look elegant! And a mane of very coarse silver hair!).

Ohbytheway: "*Your name wouldn't happen to be* Pluvus?!". But he only shook his head. Furrowed his brow, too (and Thalia, next to me, did likewise.) / Why?: He was a notorious felon; just barely tolerated now! Spiteful and sly to the nth degree: sworn enemy of rangers! — / Oh yes? : and *I* was to have handed *him* a note? Uriah Uriah cluck cluck cluck?: No sir, my dear Colonel, not me! (Stuck my hand into the sand, playful-like, and pushed the letter-cylindrette as deeply down as I could: rest in peace!).

Craftsmen, the veterans; cumbrously lazy in work and play: one of them whittling a piece of celtis wood into whiphandles (told me in confidence, that when he had a lot of time on his hands, he'd even make small flutes). But the stuff was also immensely hard; tough, difficult to split. / Another fashioned back-scratchers out of bits of cactus: cutting down the thorns to grater-size; and cutting them off altogether at the handle end: voilà! (Too rough for me. But if it were used as a curry-comb?). The next one made lances. — "Where d'you get these 10 yard rods from?!". Whereupon they took me along

to the agave plantation: The blue-green leaves growing to three metres long (heavens, you really can't call them 'leaves' anymore!), and ten inches thick: for food; for roofing, "When we build permanent homes — for a few months." / The thorns?: they make the arrow tips. (And nails if necessary). / The fibres, the sisal hemp?: linen, rope, rough fabric. (The root, finally, for medicinal purposes; laxative: "And how!").

Yes, and at the right time this giant of a plant put forth these 10-yard long 2-inch thick flower shafts! (Then you waited cunningly till datelike fruit was formed on top, and collected that as a bonanza).

Here: but you can also do this. Curious, I leant over the hip-high, arm-wide leaf-crater. "As soon as the flower shaft shows, you scoop out the topmost bud: you then get the hollow filled with juice every day for months." (And had to taste a drop right away — ? — a trifle insipid and sweet, what?: "But certainly rich in sugar, and nourishing. For the kiddies, especially." : "Oh, everybody takes to it!". / And then it came to me: that's how Pulque is made! If you ferment it. — But here they didn't seem to know about that (and I'd have to be careful about teaching them such things; it's a happier life without booze! In theory.).

Apropos liquor? : "*What's with* the little'un? The chappie who got stung awhile ago?" He was still not quite all there, but in much better shape. Solemnly, I took possession of the Gin=bottle.

(And this hornery in fact appears to develop into a secondary male characteristic! Although no single style had yet emerged: some little fellers only sported a pair of sturdy knots that gave the appearance of prematurely receding hair. Others boasted faunish convolutions, like moorland sheep. Most in evidence were the pitch-black yard-high screwlike unicorns (which only developed at the onset of puberty: That's it, after all!).

The utensils were distributed periodically by the rangers: they were measured for leather bandoliers; the youngsters got their little nickel pliers: on principle at a full-moon ceremony. / (But these gents were not regarded as particularly benevolent deities; for the leader hinted, mysterious = laconic fashion: that numerous deaths always occurred immediately afterwards (and looked at me, pleading:? — But I countered and pointed to the gin=boy, on his wobbly legs again:?! — But he slowly shook his head in sorrow: the rangers also gave medical help at times.)

Long colourcouples hung about in the sky; only two, actually — red and yellow. (And right at the back of the field of vision, another layer, widowgrey and silent). / "Thalia?!"

She stood there trim and rarin' to travel: two red stars on her chest — one left, one right, as well befits a woman! / And the leader, too, lurched up: "I'll be coming with you till tomorrow's dawn. 'Case of residual never=nevering." / Thalia's face fell at once — dead long: was this to be our big night?! (Whilst the headman strapped with his own hands several saddlebags on himself: I wasn't altogether sorry! Spiders apart: Thalia was nice, *very* nice; but a strain withal. And besides

I was offered a ride!! : 'Sitz auf, so kannstu noch Belieben fragen!').[16]

So I asked questions to my heart's content (side-saddle throughout. Thalia trotted defiantly alongside, and shook her head in a temper when I made to stroke her in consolation. Cheered up a trace, tho, when I managed to whisper her a "Tomorrow; only you, just you!" And she pranced more gaily).

Countless caves here in Nevada?: large groups of them sometimes, all in a row, with thin hard walls? — : derelict settlements, I guess! / Aware of water: they stood still at times; blew out their cheeks, dipped faces and sniffed in the clear darkness: and on. (And fables, falbalas, fantabulations: of 'laughing springs': at which the drinker falls into helpless mirth; and can only stop when he's drunk from the next, the neighbouring, one).

"Fire on the horizon?!" : *but* it was only the stars, so magnified by vapours and clusters. / Right: a distinct halo around Venus; you could easily make out rings of colour: purple, orange; violet.

"The air is sometimes full of music. And voices." (Their own superstitiously lowered at once). / And told the tale in turns, eagerly pell-mell (for Thalia, though so much younger, knew of the event): one time, for many days, the whole tribe heard song and heartless whistling coming from a cleft in a rock. And strident sounds as from angry men: they quarrelled;

[16] See Goethe, 'Klassische Walpurgisnacht': Faust II, Scene I, line 7330.

issued orders; there were bangs, and then another screamed immediately (so loud that a stampede amongst the listeners all but broke out!) Then, after anxious weeks for the tribe, the sounds waxed ever softer: only if one held a large pointed ear very close one could still hear a sweet monotonous fluted melody, like a maiden's mouth. / (Very likely, some joker amongst the rangers had hidden a portable in the cleft rock: let there be a myth. / A daring act though; reckless, crude, irresponsible; *I* wouldn't risk anything like that! / Or maybe I already had? With my magic bottle? — Just watch out! Careful!).

: and they stiffened their legs slanting forwards! His rump now hard, and trembled so much that I would have jumped off anyway: I went to stand between the two; so; and as added precaution I held fast to the manes in the smalls of their backs, for they were snorting, seemingly about to shoot a bolt (the hair above the brows, too, had risen en brosse: undoubtedly an outward sign of fear. Or better = more cautiously formulated: some specific mode of excitement; interesting.)

For over there, in a hardly discernible shallow dip, a faint glow had begun to rise! Got brighter. Blushed pink. Taller than a man, and just as slim. / "Shush!" / Stood quite still (shape like a juniper tree; but as I said, pale red, and soundless): "Be quiet: *I* am with you!" (And silly though it sounded: their trembling subsided. They actually did rely on 'rangers' in an uncanny kind of way! But of course I was still patting flank and croup unceasingly. (My arm took a firm grip on Thalia: the feel of these things was really *too* extraordinary!).).

"No! Don't go!" She whisper = pleaded with a shudder. And so I spared myself the few steps; for it would not have appeared a sign of bravery, but merely as one of corrupt familiarity with such satanic crafts. / Will-o'-the-wisps, of course. Our domestic variety, natural gas set alight on contact with the air, and liable to burn on for hours.

But the headman, too, shook his athlete's head: "You never find a crevice in the ground; not a hole, not a pore." / (If they were a multitude and time allowed, they'd hastily pile a henge of stones around the spot after the event).

So we stood for a long while, and stared at each other. We, Brothers Three: versus a burning bush. (Still as a god of fire; with a red shock of hair. Only once did he move the tip of his head, quickly, angrily, to one side (which we took as a sign that he resented our presence)).

"The soul of the Tyrant Chairman Fórmindulls!"[17] (before I was able to explain to them what it was, burning there). / And, for my further information: "the evil spirit that created us." — "So you were created by the *Evil* spirit?" I asked full of interest; and they gazed round in astonishment: "Yes. : are you telling us you were made by a *good* 'one?'". (To which he — not for nothing the leader, athlete & thinker — added ponderously: "*Is* there a good spirit?". —. —.[18] I didn't like to answer; I didn't feel easy — never have! — in my pink skin).

On at a steady trot: the moon (I was using their 'Gow=chrómm' by now!) lifted its head and spied over the rim: soon we'd ride sleepily in yellowing worlds.

Kip down for the night?: "Quite soon. Bunch of caves ahead." — I jumped down and ran on foot (though my heart was throbbing mightily: really should have dismounted a while ago, when we were stomping uphill!) between them through the dewless night. After many a silly word it showed on the horizon:

the steep gables, high into the dawngrey. Entering the place a tin sign declared: 'Candelaria'. / He looked at me in a British sort

---

[17] An idiomatic rendering of Foreign Minister Dulles?
[18] If I interpret correctly the intricate, 'New Punctuation' now unfortunately so widely employed in the West & the US, then this combination of dashes and dots is probably supposed to represent a 'reflective pause'. — I should like to make it quite clear that I am opposed to his cult, above all to the semi-colon!

of way:[19] "What does it say, actually?". And I enjoyed mouthing him this particular wordsound; seemed to me to fit in nicely with their other neologisms.

So this was our arrival in the deserted town; we, faces overcoated in twilight. / The streets were covered with shifting sand that muted our clatter of hooves (often metre-high, blown sideways against the walls: one makes a distinction, walking streets between the long 'ahead' and the rushing 'sideways' images). The Gow=chrómm's empty face a soundless onlooker. Once a muted clap thlunked in the distance (windowframei'thewind? — "Candelaria, Candelaria" a steady accompanying murmur: the chief memorizing the name). / We went into a hot room at ground level. Where we bedded ourselves down on the sandied floor.

"Oh never here!: they've got to keep guzzling all the time, see?" (The Never=nevers): "Blood or plantjuice by the litre; or they dry out very fast." — Pulled large ears of corn from their bags and began to munch: the kernels softly churning in their molars. Thalia played herself imperceptibly closer to my side (crunching and savouring a sprig of salt: for dessert) / In the flat hot sand. / "Shadow of a Unicorn on Moonyellow": as title for a painting (or simply 'Unicorn Shadow'. — But 'Unicorn' is wrong, anyway!)

"Why: Don't you make your winter quarters here? In these deserted places?" / And she: "The White?" (is that how they revile the winter?) They coordinated their views (i.e. the leader held forth; Thalia duly inched closer): "The White? Oh, that's nogood!" / Slow reasons: "There are special voices. The treetops turn bloody and tremble. Gow=chrómm goes crooked and cold; and lies on his hollow comb back. No grass, or if there is, it's painfully hard to scratch up — nono: we prefer to emigrate, South."

---

[19] NB the meaning that 'British' has won over there since 1988. It is, transcribed, a mixture of mistrust, arrogance, reserve, trust, etcetera.

End of feed. He took another look outside, at the weather? : No; no danger of a duststorm. / The four-fold reflection of the moon felt warm (& tasted bitter, when I stole a nosh of the Boraxsands). The 'Red Patch' served as a branded dimple on its chin: surely Thalia couldn't get any closer than *this!*

The lambent pubilability of slow-low dry chat:[20] we dallied at all kinds of horseplay. In the tender silkblack hour. / The chief had stuck his head in the corner and snored emphatically (reared his brow at every soundchange though. — : "Can't make it now, Thalia!" — (And a horn like that must be quite a handicap: sleeping. — Or putting on a hat! : Must have a peep tomorrow morning and see if they have a hole in it.)). Luminous threads streamed out of the moonjet, chemical fibres. And he prowled on and on in his yellowtinted ether. Till my very brain was touched. ("Kisses at night, don't sleep tight": that's it — exactly!).

—. —. —. —. —. —

: a thick reddish odour all around: as if it emanated from their nostrils, that's how they were breathing. / (Got up sharpish to fulfill a — no, well, two! — matitutinal compulsions (Smokeboghotterfogthicketmoisthottestmud)).

"Bye-bye!" at the exit of the place: and a cactus lifted its hairy oath-taking hand: the chieftain set off at a trot: Fine Fellow, definitely! (A bunch of echoes rang back from the roseate houses, sounds extended). (At the last look-round I lit on a crooked tree, painfully sprouting on the barren soil: thus deserving a mention).

And: "Hey Thalia? How's that?: The first fresh dawning look not for me?!: Comeonoverhere, you!" so she forgot her morning browse; and more — ambled over to me; we tumbled all over ourselves, "Othalia!", (at one point I was almost standing on my head!)

[20] Probably intended as a paraphrase of clumsy love-talk; as per the original.

(But also: 'At once the restless rolling rotor stops'![21] — She looked at me in disappointment; I wasn't Her Cules after all. / Then a brainwave seemed to lift her: "Say — there are sure to be some further out!"). —

Further out; the edge of the township was already behind us. / Entr'acte: her scorching embrace: "Couldn't you stay? With me as your woman: You mount me; and we ride: Anywhere!"

The thunderstorm blew me out of that embarassement; her thoughts, too, got diverted, and we gazed at the scant combat of lightning. / Pollard willows by the creek, bundles of sabres above furry heads awaiting the crackling fuse of thunder start: a gash in the air! (Once, frozen to the spot: and now a redspanned emanation on the tree-shaft. Even she hesitated before she recognized=dismissed it).

No! riding her was out! I'd rather kiss her from up there to the Ohó; and there she stirred again (it was supposed to be an age-old centaur's trick; a chief's wives' secret; (swiftly circulated to her girlfriends by the chief's darling daughter!)).

The plain was sown with herbs 4 to 5 feet high. Sweetsmelling. Sage & others. With gleaming leaves of greeny leather. / Once we leapt together over a crevice. (First try: I held onto her mane in the small of her back; we took a running jump — at least 4 yards: hippety-hop!). / "Andlook — there are lots!"

Now choose! : Thalia in a nettlefield (looking enchanting, from the front: hard white creature hip-high in green!). (And on the flanks, too, sure thing. But she was trampling impatiently):

And mine was "the choice": that one, on the left, proffered evanescent. / The other: persistent charm, with each lubrication. / (And the hellish=third a lifelong crazy itch: now, choose!).

---

[21] Origin of quotation unbeknown to me: the author's handwriting in the margin is scarcely legible even with the aid of a magnifying glass: 'Member' (?), 'Momber(t)' (?), 'Membrin' (?).

So I chose the evanescent charm: she expertly plucked up the relevant type of nettle (her hand protected by the woof of her food-satchel — hope she doesn't confuse the species!)

"*No: you've got* to stand with your back to the tree!" (Heated smile. And I also had to fold hands behind me — "And lock your fingers quite tight together!" / Came round, facing me. Weighed it on her palm. Pulled back with relish — : and rubbeduptubstream=leafstemeverythinghelterskelter: !!!! :

"*Ffffffffffff : stop!!*" as if I'd been dipped into fire! Stamped my feet: "Stop woman!" Only now did it occur to me to undo my hands; swiftly she threw it away, greenweed and stringy-stuff. Opened her nest (and I worked away like a maniac! If only to get rid of the burning!). / (She sang my pinkplush praises and proposed afresh to abduct me.)

But first of all I'm bogged down by this fiendish thirst! (So I hurriedly staggered in her wake, through undergrowth of pine and hardwood) . . . . . . :

"*Oh: a geyser!*" : I plonked myself down, a beaker in each hand, half lame, to a two-fisted booze-up. Until I noticed the bitterness of the stuff! "Can hardly call it a *vintage* spring, eh, Thalia!" "Vintage? No, not vintage" she parries equably. / Every 5 minutes the sintercrater threw up its fountain; the third time it plumed higher: high and hot and gallbitter: "Gotta get out o' this place!"

Made what looked like detours to me; for the sun gazed=surveyed us at astoundingly varied slants: ? ! / "Yep. — We'd be there in an hour, or else!" (Laid her pretty head on my chest. And boo-hooed. 'Midst willows, poplars, elms and Celtis: "You were the first to give me that feeling!" / "No: I'll think about it always!" / "You-hoo back soon?" / Though I said "Yes" to that, I folded my lips bethoughtfully (nor did she seem to expect otherwise from deities. But rueful-resolute, 'Great Expectations',[22] wiped her face on mine.)

---

[22] Novel by Charles Dickens, 1861.

"There": at least handed her the gift of my sunglasses (I'd planned that when we got back to the wall; but with her moping so sad-inconsolubly, we embraced passionately — so I handed 'em to her right now:!)

Beaming — worldly-wise again: "Oooh You!" / Pause. (Several try-ons: no denying it was good for the eyes) / "No-one here has a pair of these!!" (Silly-owly; desired admiration without end. And skipped great hoops of gratitude: "Ohh Yoooh!!"). But then it started blowing behind me again!:

"What goes on?!" — : "That?: Flying Heads." / : So this is the mysterious 'Third Kind' mentioned yesterday! Hexapodes, for sure: but butterflies — really!

"Wanna see one close up?" : she suddenly reared up giant-tall on her hindlegs — : — : and grabbed one from its leafy nook: there!

And here I am with the beheaded (or rather, disrumped being, in my hand: definitely a human face; and so light in my palm!)

"Helloo there?!" — It rolled its eyes in terror. Bleated softsweetly (and stretched out a hand-long hollow tongue: "Heeiih . . .") / Large soundless butterfly wings. Singleclawed hooks at the outermost tips (for hanging out on slender branches? For sleep at night?). And under the chin a brace of tiny feet for sitting: that's how it had been curiously watching us from its branch.

Quite soft and elastic, this globule: I gave it a light experimental squeeze — and again the featherweight creature exhaled discomfort: "Heeh."

(But sweet faces! : An attractive mouth — wide and searing guile — and a sensual hooter setting it off: never seen her like before! (How do I conclude it's a 'she'? . . . Just had a feeling, somehow.) Enchanted, I drew the chrome=yellow mask towards me; caress its tip-top — very lightly, tenderly, of

course — and at once the feathery balloon pressed itself, fluttering, sucking against me: mmmmmm!)

"Now now, Thalia!" : for she'd wrested the creature from me, hissing with jealousy; took a swing and burst it between her little fists like a child with a paper bag: Ping! / "Now really, Thalia!!!" / But she knelt before me so — (imagine: a deer lying at your feet!) — and took me, yearning=beseeching, so=oh, into her raspberry mouth; wellnigh choked, fists imploring: so=oh=ooh! Raged petulant — gently boo-hooing: "Mine!" (add: You are) — that there was nothing for it but to forgive her (and all the while up among the cactus-crowns, the sweet monotone bleating: terribly distracting!)

Seams of fury still creasing her face: more footnotes to jealousy: it's said they gobble up the women's milk, these Flying Heads! And the first spunk of youth (while he lies sleeping). / "No; on their tongues: the females have handlong pinkish tubes" (they are the dreaded suckers!) The males have an equally long blown-up kind of penis (legend has it they oft-times lewdly make for centaurlets' behinds — : what alibis these bucolic belles dream up for themselves; (A load of old crap, of course; couldn't make it in a million years!)). / She raucously plucked a large flower-face; locked her hand round its blue throat and gave it a sadistic squeeze: whooshing-wide did the dumb beast gape open its gob: air! (And I almost expected a 'Baaah', even on this occasion: "Thalia! Come on")!

"Yes of course!" : *the Never=Nevers* loved to trap them in their nets. Also prized their 'other shape' from inside cactuses (an insectual metamorphosis, you see, like larvae? — But she couldn't make head or tail out of my expert scientific explanation). / "The Prairie-owls hunt them. And our kids like pop-shooting at 'em with their toy arrows." : "Well Thalia!" / But she only shook her cheeks, sadly: "There." — : A greyer streak on the horizon: the World's End!

(And a wrench of an au-revoir in a bushscrub: she near-tore me to pieces. Embraced me with those arms so white; plus forelegs; now all six at once! (Weighed at least 200 pounds!: "Oh Thalia!")).

One last kiss: ! : !! : !!! The like of which I'd never tasted during a long and misspent earth life! / "Ooooohh=oo=oh: oh!" and howled so that it streamed down under the sunglasses.)

Then waving goodbye: she was already far away. Once more lifted her arms: they sagged. Her hindrump trotted off with her. (And I stared after her — my arms across my chest, perplexed. It was all too much, all at once; for a simple journalist!). —

Off to the Great Wall (that's to say: to the 'End of the World'; how soon one might get used to their way of speaking! (In my fantasy I was already imagining wildlife in this steppe; with arrow and Centie-bow; nights atop Thalia celebrating the feast of tabernacles, only the stars above my cap . . . But all that was senseless; too much for one man. Best hobble along!). —).

Thrown a stone at the turret? The sentry, who was in love with his machine=gun, woke up *there*.[23] Revealed a totally bewildered and sleep-sick visage (presented himself; and directed me to the North, to the nearest big Wallstation). —

The Big Wallstation (first through a halflit echoing stonetunnel; then I was outside the wall) / : "Oh-ho; it's you?!" (and evidently *so* unpleasantly surprised!). / . — . / "Oh, just a tic: Wouldn't you maybe like a bath first?". / Sure; a pleasure.

Within the green pine-needle enamel (and he still verily sinister: had Thalia secretly taken the lifelong sort after all?!). But watch it now; I'd most likely be disposed of somehow. Or at least would be made to swear an oath for a change . . . / — Knock-knock?? — : "Yeah yeah, coming rightaway!"

---

[23] In reference to the well-known play by William O'Nail, 'The Soldier's Progress'.

"Well now." (and the Doctor=Director visibly relieved): "We have orders from Washington to put you under oath: Raise your hand please . . . (and called to the ante-chamber: "Er-Flushing? : Come in here a min, willya. So you can sign as witness." / Forthwith shambles in the lanky lassie, weary and all; obviously paid no attention; but proceeded to sign everything without demur. (And that damned urtication stung again immediately, even with this wallflower; what a drag!).).

But now, having done with oath-taking — (on Interworld 187 by the way: for publication in dead languages only: remarkably mild!) — he became quite civilized. One (= we) smoked and drank Bora=Bora.[24]

Now gave information freely, to each of my questions./: "Yes, just so. 'Hexapody' is the word alright. — On the one hand with insects: hoofed creatures on t'other: with retention/adaptation of the arms, as the case may be; yep." (Arm*less* throwbacks were "currently being eliminated — uh=painlessly, of course": lovely expression!). (And I generalized significantly: stags, tapirs, female elephants, rhinos, hippos, dwarfed mountain goats. : Or some species of giraffes, high up aloft a sad silly human head. (But perhaps it was supra=horned; with pince-nez; and feeling fine). / Shaggy pony species in the North; with rough bushy hair between the breasts.)

"Wolves as enemies?!" : he only laughed: "Well, look here: I wouldn't want to be a wolf and find myself amongst a pack of Centaurs! They'd remove my appetite in no time! Imagine: hooves sledge=hammering blows, fore & aft; Hand=brandishing bows, arrows, serrated swords, lances, clubs, cudgels . . . and that horn on the head?: merci beaucoup!!"

"No, unfortunately not!: Deep in the southlands negroid nomads are found. — There were, as you know, three races to start

---

[24] The new nonalcoholic fruit drink; tastes quite like the old 7-Up.

with: derivative of Whites, Negroes, Indians. Of which White and Indian have as good as amalgamated./ — ? : Yeah; right enough: it happened — at first by chance, then directed — with Grant=Gazelles: *very* happy combination!" / And bent forward from yellow swivelchair: "What?: You've spotted a zebroid mongrel? : But we must eliminate that at once!" (Made notes with flying fingers: OhgodamIthentobe . . . : accessory to the death of that gorgeous creature?! He quickly noticed my concern, and assiduously reassured) / : "Oh you *must* see that! We keep medical watch over all the troupes: the brutally deformed; vicious males; those with excessively= large horns — that could lead to difficulties in delivery — are mer-ci-less-ly shot down!" (By blowpipe: a minuscule glass-arrow loaded with poison): "As far as possible we want to preserve them for us, the human race! — That heavy unicorn — which *can* cause brain-involution — ; or the — albeit unavoidable — rough grazing tongue that impedes speech, and has already changed it somewhat: cause us *great* anxieties!" / : "Surely you understand that."

Yehyeh sure, understood, but.

Further details: gestation period? : "174 days on average. At age three they're ready to breed." / Average life-span?: "12 to 20. The ancient ones get real 'wise' — in the socratic sense, to be sure — and sometimes, though *very* rarely, they even learn to read and write." / How many? : "Well, our rangers know just about every unit, and estimate the total population at around =uh — 6.000. Of whom 700 are blacks." (Strictest segregation of the races. Census and surveillance carried out partly by air, unobtrusively, I had noticed that; partly by field-work: "Oh, you know." Yes.).

"Ohyeah, one more thing, Doctor, how about that?: is it regarded as sodomy? — I mean: in case a ranger should *happen* to-um=fall in love with a centauress?" / He tugged thoughtfully at his chin (employing the index-finger to squash down his

sizeable nose): "Hum." / "Hmm, of course you've hit on a problem here: there certainly *is* a gap in our legislation. — Which is further aggravated by the following facts: *Human*-males and Centaur-*females*: a barren combination — that much has been tested. B-b-but!: Centaur-*males* and Human-*females*: something can come out of that, for sure! How many elderly=lecherous millionairesses — by bribing one or other of the guards — have got themselves smuggled into the Hominid Strip and been inseminated by Centaurs! : And I don't have to tell you how *they* are built!"

"No, no, you see, the problem in question has only become acute with us, with the guards personnel here. And the common law rule here — though not yet codified — is: it's *not* sodomy. Ergo *not* punishable." (And I was considerably relieved. While all I uttered was a nonchalant "H=hm").

"Quite true: the breasts of the females are getting smaller. Through natural selection: they become less of a hindrance to galloping. The covering epidermis firmer: quite correct." / "They address each other as 'brother-in-law' — to be on the safe side, I suppose: for relations between the sexes are relatively unstable."

And dry laugh, in lots of little spurts: "Yes=yes! — Well; can reveal it to you; sworn in now." (In spite of which he retained his restrained smoker's pause): "Yeahwellthat's=tosay, 'Fórmindulls': 50 years ago this Secretary of State for Foreign Affairs had advised decisively to continue with atomic tests . . ." / And I'd already interspersed an enlightened "Oh=really?!: 'For=Min' — that stands for 'foreign' and 'minister'?! — : Ohyeah. Hmm. Now a few things are coming more clear." (But of course this was the vital clue; you live and learn!). / 'Gow' — another he didn't know. 'Chromm' was the Celtic 'krumm' — 'crooked' — though why this should derive from the Gaelic of all things was another unknown: "Coincidence, most like. Apparently a forester of Irish extraction intervened."

"*Well of course ethnologists* have struck a rich vein here. They rub their hands with glee every time there's another custom they can file: sure, it *is* of great interest! / For instance, did you know *this:* That old and ill specimens always withdraw to very specific places when they're about to die? Into deathvalleys, where veritable boneyards have come into being?: 'Centie=cemeteries' our folks always call 'em. / Or water. Their A1 priority — understandably: where streams run in different directions, bifurcations or watersheds, they put up cairns — where it's forbidden ever to settle. / No noooo; in winter they migrate southward: Arizona, California, Sonora. What do you mean? : we get *here — in this place!*" (stabbed his blotter with his forefinger; very convincing) : "January temperatures down to minus 38 degrees!" (For summertime a corresponding plus 42 had been recorded). / "Yes=yes: in emergencies we provide drinking troughs. But that's only happened once in practice — when a daredevil troupe in search of new grazing-grounds had ventured too far into the Ralston Desert. They're normally so mobile and well-oriented that they can always get to the nearest watering place: 150 miles in 24 hours is what a Centie in good health can manage — if he wants to."

Inclined his head in assent: "*Snakes* and biting insects we've destroyed; by means of contagious poisons; and irradiation: first of all, we had to create favourable environmental conditions. The difficulties are vast enough anyhow." / "Mainly that, like any herd, they have a tendency — congenital to their equine half — to collective fright. Triggered off by noises, explosions, etcetera. Appalling dread overwhelms them: the entire tribe, one hundred of them, race off like crazy, and nothing can stop the stampede; they'll collide with a rockface or shatter themselves to pieces down a ravine — at the very least, it results in the most annoyingly complicated fractures!" (and shook his head disapprovingly, as if he personally had to repair the damage).

"Yes, sure, we do that too! D'you think it's for nothing that we're their guardians and helpmates?!" / And thus (as I had intended) provoked, gave an account of their 'tasks': "At first; in the very beginning; we tried to disguise 2 of us as a Centie. — You may well laugh: just like a panto-horse, like those unemployed of former times, or at parades. And the man in front went into action: did inoculations, made plaster-casts, removed skin-parasites, injected a hormone here, a hormone there. / Till at last they got accustomed to our appearance. Now they call us 'rangers' — although I personally don't appreciate that silly name *at all!* — and accept tools etc. as a godsend. . .: I beg your pardon?" / What I'd murmured was "One man's garbage is another man's heaven-sent food." He took it personally, this Big Chief of the Rangers, and twitched his nose contentedly, once.

The 'Religion of the Centaurs'? : first he made his mouth into a funnel, then relaxed it in dismissal: "They don't have one. Apart from an historically determined animism. Sublimated, of course: our very presence contributes enormously to the formation of a theological system. So. This is a natural development, bbut it can't happen without coercion: I repeat can *not*!" / Impressive. Sat both his hands on the plate-glass in front of him, intending to push himself upwards. But remained on his backside and listened, his face intense:...?...?: "Well this *is* —— *most* important: Mr. Winer!"

(For I'd told him about the spider-battle; and how I cured the little one who'd been bitten: he was all ears: nodded at the details I supplied: and sometimes moved his lips in soundless unison: "Really? — Aha!") . / Then began to explain "You realize of course — we know all about this! We've autopsied plenty of dead specimens; but we've always arrived at the scene too late: by the time a runner gets the news to the wall and we get

someone there it's all over and done with; that stuff takes effect within a quarter of an hour! — Say, you *wouldn't* have any of it left?" / I obligingly dragged the bottle out of my luggage. He pulled the cork, poured into a glass dish, was on the point of dunking his tongue . . . but then something seemed to occur to him (and this looked *real* cute: this pointed-beardface right opposite me, hovering above the plate-glass, tongue still poke=stretched out (the thinking had made him forget to pull it in); the grey=furrowed brow; the strained forehead; eyes espying a certain something in mid-table . . .).

His tongue-flesh slowly slid back into place. He clapped his mouth shut. His face ascended once again to its normal elevation (and looked so ingenuous, it was hard to believe it could belong to a Doc=Director): "Uh=Flushing! — Excuse me just one moment Mr. Winer — have Dr. Fielding come over — yes, At=The=Double!" (Also murmured something about 'examine thoroughly . . . Composition . . . Extraordinarily significant . . .')

"*Well, so, as far as* you could ascertain, that — helped? — Hm.", thus attempting to bridge that long-lasting pause. (By then I'd told him five times in constantly=varying versions; *and* confirmed; *re*confirmed; and yet again did nod yeah*yeah*; and the chemical doctor *still* hadn't turned up — till at last he seemed to make up his mind — made up a mien of super- =importance, and got started on a lengthier case report (I didn't want to see what he was scribbling; no doubt a fervent little prayer. Or, more likely, incomprehensible, rune-like scratchings. — So: did him the favour and gazed discreetly out of the window).

Therethat=therewas=surely — : "*Centaurs?!*" : *was I wrong* — But he assured me — glad of the diversion, that I could trust my own eyes: "We'll be going down presently. — Aha: please, don't be shy please?!"

"Doctor Fielding — Mister Winer of the 'Kalamazoo Herald'. — Now see here Doc, have a peep at this bottle: it's Gin. Would you make a thorough analysis — for real, all the trimmings; and sort out every single component? Because, you see it is *that: . . . .?"*

But Dr. Fielding, long, pale, thin and dry, had long since lifted the stopper; sniffed; snorted; poured down into his left palm and bedded a coated tongue in it (eyes concentrate=portcullised: i.e. did *not* see the boss's excited finger-signals; instead talked out and over his mouldy taste-organ in a practiced slur): " — $C_2 H_5 OH$=Derivate." — He tasted and mused; all his features united round his mouth; his forehead became alarmingly large and smooth: "Aconitumdigitalisbelladonna" he said very fast; opened his eyes portentously: "And a few more things — I proceed with the analysis: when will the Director require the results?" But he only waved in assiduously suppressed fury: "Thanks, Thanks! — Uh-tomorrow morning; please!" (The head of the white tube bowed and clicked heels, and betook his long legs 'towards analysis'; and whilst the door behind the automaton fell shut again, I made the poor joke of sotto voce=memorizing: "Wolfbane; Foxglove: Deadly Nightshade." . But he too had regained his balance: "Traces" he said shortly: "Unavoidable in distillation. Besides, the man periodically suffers from Korsakov=Psychosis. — Come along, please."

Along many corridors, white stairs: "Well uh=unfortunately we know scarcely anything about that: how far ahead the Russians are! Of course they *have* got the whole of Europe for their Hominid field research, all the way back, as far as the Urals."

"It's one blessing for us the Germans & Japs are gone"[25] I said forcefully: "A world war without those two wouldn't have been the same to be sure!" And he turned to me bowing enthusiastically. "I *quite* agree! Absolutely. Nono: this last uhum — rationalization — uh — was in the last analysis to be welcomed: how this has contributed to the spread of reason in the rest of the world! — Well, it is *said* — I don't know; I'm repeating rumours: which as a scientist, one certainly shouldn't: — that the gentlemen in Shemipalatinsk had been concentrating on *aquatic* forms . . . ." — lifted his finger-bunches shoulder-high; and let his head sway to and fro. / Anyway — there's lots more to come! Everything in a state of flux!: We'll live to see *quite* a nice little lot yet!" he concluded with shining eye, and gave the bridge of his specs an animated shove.

"Oh, quite a simple aviary!" We'd halted in front of the wire cage: tall and wide as a mid-town apartment block. Iron railings at 2 yards distance all the way round. And I slouched my elbows atop, amazed, (head in handprop: I felt as if I were in the zoo!)

The aviary: "No. We call them 'Flying Masks': for there are certain fixed recurring typological cycles." (Differentiation by gender; males have about half a dozen 'Facial Expressions'; females considerably more: "That can decidedly be varied & stabilized according to our wishes by means of selective breeding as to attractiveness, hair style of the females and-such-like: voice especially!: some of them, if they're kept in small cages, already emit a kind of singing sound; yeah." And we spurred our glances to range across the vast expanse of mesh.

[25] I do not hesitate to translate even this part literally: quite apart from my duty as a sworn translator, and my personal feelings as a Germanic survivor (1 of the remaining 124), it is after all historically important to preserve such attitudes — not at all rare or uncommon in the North and East — in print. Later centuries may judge between Goethe and 'Fórmindulls'. I refrain from making any comment, lest I be accused of personal animosity.

Planted the trees inside?: "*No.* Built round 'em; the other way would have taken much too long." / Mostly giant cacti? : "There's a good reason for all that: let's go straight over to the lab, OK?"

In the lab: Oh my dear Fórmindulls! — Only now did I grasp the full meaning of the metamorphosis!

And the whitecoated girl technician fluently explained and demonstrated: Here in this succulent — ("You have to look right against the light!") I recognized a crouching quiet dark kernel. "Yes, right." / Here's the X-ray. / "And this is how they look in natura." ('in natura' was good; she meant 'in proof-spirit'; occupational semi=soullessness). — Length and thickness of a good old cucumber. Deadwhite: result of living in plants — and what kind of an 'inner life' for that host plant; worse than a tapeworm! — Darkly speckled on the trachial termini only. Pale embryo=face; a transparent skin covered the eyeballs: evil sucker! / "They live through this phase for two years in oily plants — the only ones that afford them sufficient shelter. — Pardon? — : No; the host does *not* die! An entasis is usually formed in the affected area." Or encysted tumours : no. / "The eggs? : are produced exactly as with insects, by pairing, in the imago. And a piercing terebra erected for the purpose and immediately discarded, punctures the flesh of the plant. (Where 'the appropriate development' proceeded to begin).

"*Here: here you can see it repeatedly.*"; and led me to another cactus-stump: one of its erect members had burst (the wound, however, had already patiently cicatrized into a yellowish-dry scar: good.); and in the corner of a fork did motionlessly hang the pale yellow cocoon, 2 spans long. / "Of course, one can kill off the pupa in simmering water and use the thread in textile manufacturing; each one yields over half a pound of thin, very firm yarn: here; my straps are made of it": she artlessly pulled aside the shoulder of her clinician's overalls: and I looked at the wide straps of her brassiere, shivering, mon Dieu (and that's all they wear. Not surprising in this heat!). — : "Ohyes: your trousers, too, Sir, are made of the material." (and nodding he slapped his thigh with a nonchalant hand).

"How long do they live then, the" (I conquered my disgust; gave in and finally let out the infamous expression; courage, my friend): "the 'Flying Masks'?" / That depended; they were eagerly concerned with lengthening the life-span: "2 to 3 months as things stand at the moment, i.e. here; in captivity. Outside, in open wildlife, they have too many enemies: owls; the few species of surviving small predatory birds: and above all those sodding arachnids!" / They, the spiders, were *extremely* unpopular here (and quite-right too, as my personal experience testifies): they caught the larvae, drill-boring into the cactus stems with their proboscis — which they did anyway — deeper and deeper if they sniffed the scent, right down the larva-body, which they greedily sucked dry. Even gulped down the pupae. And the imagos they'd stalk with their nets: "And then they're so *stupid* with it — or rather, sex-mad & inept that, though they've excellent vision, they go straight for the male; whether there's a spider's net in the way or not."

"Ergo, let's get rid of these Never=Nevers!". And grimly they nodded heads: "We'd dearly love that: if only we knew the magic formula! — But it's not, unfortunately, that simple; they're mighty mighty tough. We've had some very sweet successes — notably aided by the Centies — and managed to stomp the beasts off way up North. But they already seem to be adapting quite easily to the cold primeval Canadian forests: a vermillion=furcoated species has evolved, with an incredibly hard proboscis which can bore deep into the saptubes of tree trunks . . . ." (Both of 'em sighed a deep sigh in team rhythm): "There's plenty-plenty work yet for us."

And exit through the other door: we stood there surrounded by the vast station=sportsground. And instantly entranced, I had my hands on my hips: Man, what speed!²⁶ (And he too, by my side, nodding and enthusing all over his beaming Director's=dial: "Any takers for keeping up with that, eh?!")

The Centies it was — racing each other!!: Now they were four abreast waving fleetfoot over the last hurdle near us at the finishing post. Heads in a long forward stretch; in their right the shortish whip (with which they began thrashing their own behinds! Suddenly, on the inside track, the giant bay, Man of War, shot forward, as if a gigantic hand had propelled him from be=aft: 10 yards, 20, 30!! — : (and lance=tore the tape with his horn=point!))!

Now for the man with the stop-watch!: And he too was agreeably excited: "A one-thirty-one-point-fourteen mile! And that only in training: can you *imagine* what times'll be snatched on Sports Day!" / "Yeah=eah: that's not an easy trick to pull, breasting the tape with your actual horn. Saves at least another three-hundredth of a second!" / But you couldn't get them used to sulkies for trotting: "Your Centie brooks no yoke!" had been a Chief's pronunciamento: the Centie's pride I prize! — (And only the most dearly beloved or venerated persons were allowed a ride: that's me!)

Walking along: "Oh, the tournaments are very popular, hordes of contestants. — Of course, we don't stand a chance at sprinting and hurdling; these are separate events. Longjump likewise." / And where could they compete? : "Well=uh: weight-putting, for instance; there the chances of winning are even. From a standing position, of course — ! 'Cause if a centie — even if the putting-circle is ever so small — were to spring=release the fourfold force of the legs — Oh wow!" (Thus, generally speaking, all throwing events, in particular: javelin, discus, weight).

---

[26] The following scenes are typically American! We outcast Germans would presumably have seen to it that they learned Greek, and generally remained natural.

"Or here"; and this time I had to prop up my face with both hands: The B Teams were doing their football training with each other! / (Get used to that many legs, for a kick-off . . . .) / An assyrian-bearded Centaur was stopping the ball with his chest: it slid down him obediently. Lightningquick he put a hoof on it — glanced 'round —: and lobbed it straight ahead (where his centaur-forward instanter=instepped it over with his right *hind* leg (sic) — but the more than seven feet tall human defence had already leapt across the trajectory, headed it back to his goalie (who hugged the orb in his fatherly arms; neatly evading a dappled one about to fair=tackle him, and kicked it wide into the other half:!)).

"Yeah, but don't you have to take the same factor into account: that their sprinting is so much faster?" But he'd already brushed that away with his hand: "That's more than compensated for by the fact: that their goalie is that much clumsier!" (and, thoughtfully): "A Centaur team with a human goalie —theoretically — unbeatable! Why, those guys shoot penalty kicks?! : Recently one of our goalies had his skinchest bust wide open by one of 'em!" / (Stop; one more thing: "About heading?: the advantage of a horn!": "Oh sure, that's right rough on the balls.").

"When?" (the Games): "Oh dear, you'll be long gone by then. In another fortnight. Exclusively internal affair."

"Prizes?" — *: "Varied.* — Mostly things that can be used by the winners' whole tribe: a shiny aluminium bucket; 3 steel speartips; our training course not only improves their physical fitness, but their mental qualities too: fast reactions; decision making; fighting spirit — all benefit us in our fight with the arachnid forces: andsoonandsoon." (Man proposes, Fórmindulls disposes).

Glassblue evening edged in gold: the Centaurs and opponents exchanged goodly handshakes (whereupon they were channelled through the gate, back to their territory). / "But of course: 8 in all." / (That's to say: underpasses below the hominid strip that connects the two halves of the United States; from Mazatlan to Fort Churchill. Flights over only at very great heights, more than 50,000 feet; on account of these panic fears).

And listened to the smart youngsoldier — : ? — : "Oh good: Your baggage has just arrived by postal rocket. I'll have it delivered to your room." And going on from there, mine grandiloquently booming host (a painfully bad impression had to be wiped out; you could say that again!): "Come on, you *must* lie down for a few hours! Get some rest. The machine to Eureka doesn't leave till three-thirty tomorrow morning. And first of all, have a decent meal: Please!"

The Canteen: if you please: He dined, quite the patriarch, amongst his assistants and GI's. Waved genially betimes in the direction of some faraway table. Or laughed at a tamely servile joke: in my domain wit shan't go unrewarded! / (Anyway, what's cooking? Not rattlesnake in hemlocksauce again, I hope; mad-dog smoked ham, larded with scorpions . . . .) / But no: the food was really good. Simple and nourishing; lots of meat. Just a slight poke with the fork and another meatball cottoned on to it. (And the WAC waitresses in that new frosted-glass-coloured irridescent stuff[27], arms like thin rainbows, smiled indefatigably: eat, drink and be merry, the enemy is at the Gate!).

"And this is your room!": he opened in person the door (painted glossy white on the outside); and smartly eased in with me from behind (responsible hotelier, autopsy bent, to convince himself that his honoured guest wants for no comfort. — "Right. — : Well.").

[27] Which has nothing to do with our dear German dead; on the contrary, to be understood in term of 'irisation'.

[28] Mask=linen; this has consequently become the standard technical term for textiles made from the threads of the chrysalis of the 'Flying Masks'.

"*I've had them pack a blanket* — quite a plain one — made of 'mask=linen'[28] — with your baggage" (and at the same time unceremoniously checked my belongings, what?! But I guess I had to get used to expecting that on such a trip). (And his present, too, gave me the shivers; but I forced myself to gnash my teeth courteously, until he seemed satisfied with the effect.) / "The value, for the connoisseur, lies in the material of course, not in the workmanship. — And here:": beaming, he handed over the mighty tome with both hands:! The yellow-red spur of his beard rose up proudly (and I had to admit, however unwillingly, what with his grey-specked bushy eyebrows and the remnants of steel wirewool hair, he looked quite cute), as he explained: "We do employ various draughtsmen here too; painters. And so we've produced these coloured lithographs — a limited edition; for the handful of interested parties: numbered and signed, yes, sure: all the more or less established kinds of masks to date! In addition there are enlarged photos of some particularly interesting though not yet stabilized varieties:".

I politely leafed through a few plates — : — : and they really were masterly. Very clear and distinctive. Unmistakeable likenesses. / "Well=yes, with the *proviso* that one such portrait represents the likeness of several thousands" he corrected; his arms comfortably folded over his chest.

(And striking faces amongst them, oh yeah: a sombre Timon's mask; sullen furrows on his brow, a bitter crooked mouth, mid=grey hair. / I naturally took a peek at far more females — no fear of me denying my sex!):

"*Nefertiti!*": "Yes. Bred quite deliberately." he continued: "pity they've become ombrophobes[29]; can't keep 'em indoors." / (Not 'keep them indoors'? : they've really got a nerve! Or better: totally insensate. / He looked me over — 'slyly' I felt; or was I wrong? — : "Which one do *you* like best?").

[29] Shadow-hater.

Thus compelled once more to lift the infamous folio in front of my nose — (best imagine it's a 'Gallery of American Beauties'. Useful for later on, too.)

"*Hmmmm.*" : a puffed-up babyface mouth in a pinched smile, and a repulsively rotund brow ("Our 'Mona Lisa': a successful likeness, definitely, what!") — Yes; pity. Even when I was a boy, you could have coupled me with her and there would have been nothing doing! (I hope those guys haven't gone in for imitating more portraits: what an idea!!).). / Or then again, perhaps *not*: after all, it's an ideal of beauty shared by quite a number of people; upon which they systematically refine away and produce an entire line! And did the same, after all, for Nefertiti. — So this thing, like every other under the moon, had at least its 2 sides. Though I wasn't pleased with either!)

(*Ugh, what's it matter anyway; let's end* the scene. So's the guy splits and I can doss down): "*This* one, I'd say." (She looked the spitting image of the Sumerian Queen Shub-ad, for whom I'd had the hots as a schoolboy. — And it was her, too: I hope he was satisfied now!).

"*But with pleasure!*" : *strode nimbly* to the bedside table and dialled: "Uh=Flushing? — Yeahd'youhearme?: Number 18: one:eight. / Right! / — Better still!"; and turning to me again, his mouth smiling cordially: "I'll take the liberty of having her installed here overnight, if I may?"

I sure must have looked amazed; 'cause he rubbed his hands with glee: "Well, you wouldn't have thought we worked *that* fast, what?! — I sure noticed how you took your time; and calmly selected a difficult type . . . . Ah=nonono!" (I'd raised my hands in protest): "No, it suits me fine that you put us to the test — entirely without prompting: you'll have to testify to that! It will do the public good to hear for once that we do solid work here! There's such a lot of utter nonsense being talked by laymen; so many horror stories circulated by certain interested factions: *I've* been wanting long since for a sensible, open-minded chap" (so that's me: touched, hand on heart, I bowed — what else to do?! / Just bring on your bird: I'll take a sleeping pill, so's I don't hear or see!).

Miss Flushing: in her hand a mini-cage (but large enough for the inmate to hop one up one down a bar. Also a troughlet of honeyed scented water).

"*I wish you a good night's rest* Mr. Winer. — And regret I have to bid you farewell for now —" (a long time since I'd performed such heartfelt pawshakes!) — "You *will* be called in good time: 3 a.m. on the dot — you'll make sure of that eh=Flushing." (And she made a note of it, looking important, on a shorthand pad hanging from her belt.).

Sitting on the edge of the bed. Gape at Queen Shub-ad. (They'd even hung those sophisticated double hoops on her ears. Made of something yellow, featherlight; the appendage didn't seem to bother her.)

Then the humour of the situation loomed up, after all. I propped my chin into the cleft fork of thumb and forefinger, for a longish conversation. And asked: "Well your Majesty? How are things?". / No answer. Only the eyes in her numb sensual visage started flickering — and only then did it occur to me that the poor chick was probably mightily terrified! (But that's not the first thought that occurs on meeting such a charming lady. (As a man!)).

So I flashed her a gentle smile, as reassuring as I knew; nodded like a good little boy. (But then Satan tickled me after all; and I carefully pushed my little finger through the wires:?).

"*Oooh!*" : quite high and startled. Jumped cautiously and delicately onto the higher bar, further away. Waited. Her dark eyes grew calmer; bolder too; the mouth fuller (exactly like that Sumerian broad!). / Came down again. Sniffed it (while her depraved nostrils flared!). Carefully opened her mouth, and let a hollow tube of pink tongue slowly undulate out: around my fingertips ... (its inside surface was slightly rough, a dainty suction, I felt — getting stronger, aah. But not disagreeable).

Interrogated my watch: "What time?":[30] "Twentytwo-sixteen" murmured the lazy alto I'd had installed (maybe I would have done better to take the soprano; this one sounded too damn sexy). / That late? So I withdrew my finger from the Queen of the Night — "Oooh!" she made, unwilling, put out. — And stood up.

Off to the shower in the corner; take off my clothes which I threw nonchalantly over the stool (and stretch my weary bones. Put my hands behind my ears). . . . . . .

: But now she began to get wild, real mad, seeing me like this!! Jumped to and fro; clung to the bars: "Oooohhh!" (and the tone had got throatier, darker: "Oohhhh!"). Stretched her tonguesheath as long as she could, and further, offering herself: "Ohh-ho: hoh: hohh!". / So I grew thoughtful again, despite my fatigue. While playing the shower=spout around me; feeling the thin silver=snake slither and spurt on my skin, constantly changing the water's temperature the while: that, quite decidedly, would have been sodomy! (Or perhaps they took a different attitude to this, as well? And systematically extended it: so that every soldier in the ranks, say, had his own 'Flying Mask' in his room? ('Cause there weren't enough WACs to go round. For sure.). ("What a world we live in!" — my great great=uncle would have muttered, no doubt. And now I recalled the long forgotten German writer who even then, 1790 or thereabouts, fan=zithered[31] of 'Flying

---

[30] It was a 'speaking watch' which had been quite common up there for some time now, although it is rather less popular here. The latest contraptions answer, as you know, only when 'their master' asks them; plus a male preference for women's voices has come into vogue. And vice versa.

Heads': 'Aristipp' the book was called; not a bad job either. *And* — pyschologically *very* sharp — the old master (Wieland's the name, right!) had a woman, an A:1 doll — nay, a noble courtesan — develop the theme and the play on the ideas.))*.

However, he hadn't imagined it like this then, in the Happy Teens[32]: He'd run rings round us all now! —

Dark & abed: she was still plaintive (but quieter now; low and melancholy (and my pill was working like a dream. I was just about riding off like in reverse (like a wind flopping down, exhausted, at the weeding of the potato fields: does she want to be let out?: take her to the window to fly by night? (But that spells difficulties for sure. (Wi' the Director...)))).

— —

"Yeah?! — : *Uh* — : *huh."* : i.e., the discreet "Hello?: Charley!"=phone call. (Diverse seductive girlvoices on tape: they must've recorded it last night, special: *very* thoughtful; just like back home with Ma.) / And again, how nice, the familiar admonishing woman's voice, quite the youngwife all lovingly=concerned: We must move on.: "Three o'clock, Charley. You've gotta get up. And breakfast ready=already downstairs: Come along please!". (And then the same chat over again; and again; increasing by just a shade each time in volume; the wife-nagging, getting more insistent — hard cases were resigning to have themselves pre-recorded shrewish Xanthippoid curses installed).

[31] New verb formation from 'fancy', and more contemptuous than the usual 'fantasize'.
* Christoph Martin Wieland's novel 'Aristipp' (1790) inspired Arno Schmidt to 'invent' the Flying Heads, as well as some of the verbal innovations used in this book. Tr.
[32] Now customary collective term for the centuries before 2000 (= Twenty-Hundred!) Is supposed to refer — half scornfully, half enviously and sentimentally — to the 'teenage-years' of our planet. Whereas it is after all still very debatable — to coin a phrase — if the 'mature age' will be the happier one.

The mask also awoke (she'd had her wings folded forward to sleep; over her eyes, so that only nose, mouth chin remained visible). Grumpily wiped her eyes on her wings (using the little clawhooks on the tips as cleaning-paws; for things like combing, for instance — how wisely that too has been arranged by God! (Or Fórmindulls: I shall probably never boast a 'fear-free soul' as the racy general's motto will have it.). / And the mask pushed forward a ravishingly unqueenly mug; like a filmstar's rehearsed-surprised "Ooh!" — and suddenly produced an early morning trill from the top through an entire octave, "Ooorr-lll !" : *what* more! —

A long male stride without. A military knock:?! / "OK!: I'm a = comin!"

And another who was half a head taller'n me (all handpicked guys, sure!): the Sarge. / I flung a final backward = halflook into the room: another addition to the many images I had to drag around with me (and this one guaranteed unforgettable!) — Well. there's an end to that too: *some* comfort!).

"*Uh = um. — Tell me — —* " (hesitant, so's he doesn't get me wrong): "Is there anything I can do for her?" (shoving my chin towards Queen Shub-ad over there): "She took a real power of trouble — sang me to sleep good an' hunky-dory — what?". / He smiled faintly = knowing. But at once became clipped-to-earth again: "Hardly. — Cela ne sent rien: ces Papillons là. — : they *are* being fed alright . . ." and he shrugged his broadly uniformed shoulders. / (Well: Farewell, Oh Queen. — And she followed us with distrustful glances from her slender bar).

Through corridors: "Are you French, then?" : "Canadian: Raoul Mercier. (From Rivière du Loup; on the Saint Laurent. And we jabbered happily away in French, to get acquainted, till we reached the canteen).

Yesterday's diningroom: a small table already re-laid. / "But do help yourself M'sieur Mercier!" (And bye the bye he too started to demolish crisp rolls and appetizing sandwiches. My invitation had not been devoid of ulterior motive: in case they'd slipped a shot of hemlock into the coffee again!) / And a bleached blonde was already radiantly beaming behind the counter. Came forward too; navigated her torso through shoals of tables. Handed over a sandwich-package like *so* big: "Your packed lunch!" — and bared her biting equipment: one tooth gold, the next white and so on (the reverse pattern continued in the lower jaw.[33] But I only bowed absently=sitting tight: ain't no use, baby; Thalia's blonde was singularly more interesting!). —

The ocean of concrete seemed infinite in the arena of the night. About our light-cone: ten yards wide, twenty high, the yellow cornet of fog stood motionless. (Far far behind to the left stood another, identical, but already quite small; you'd have to step through that wall of ours to see it). / Mercier already sat at the controls; and I proceeded to hand in my knapsack (which he put in the back). Then lowered moi-même underneath the ogival shape of plexiglass and struts (and rightaway arrange limbs: forward and to the right; not to get in his way; so).

Just the two of us?: and he nodded proudly: "Nothing but confidential papers and drugs" (merely a couple of medium-sized briefcases squat at the back, in the luggage space). / The seat was springy, red leather and white steel — and already tilted backwards: and so he accelerated. / Then vibrated more gently. / And we lightly shot ahead.

"Oh the few miles to Eureka?: We'll get there before sunrise!" The steering wheel began to describe its arc in his mighty fists; calmly; and back again with minute=control strength: now we were in an asphalt stream (racing madly away beneath us; up left the half moon always with us: lashed by black branches, speared by broken jet lances, the Invulnerable: colliding with

---

[33] So the above has apparently definitely been adopted in the field of cosmetics; the colours are optional; however gold, black and red are the most consistently favoured.

ebony columns, ripping leafy nets, whorls of liquorice, melanisms — : and again it had caught up with us: did marvellous time, the bowlegged one!)

And Mercier, though no gossip, obviously had something on his Sergeant's mind: "You're going to pay a visit to the 'Egghead Republic'[34] M'sieur? — I just happened to hear about it yesterday from Miss Flushing — " (was that 'his' broad? Well, tastes differ madly, as is well known; maybe her visage blossomed after office hours) — : "I=um: have a brother there. He's a painter on a three-year scholarship."

"Oh, but surely not Louis Sébastien Mercier!?": He of the 'Rise of the White Board' and the 'World Bow'?" / He nodded proudfaced into the straight night: that's the one! / "Gosh, c'est intéressant! — Yes, of course I'll give him your regards: what d'you want me to tell him?" (So touching — simply the usual: he was doing fine. Mother was still alive, ailing as per always — but that didn't mean anything; her children were used to her hinting — for the past 35 years: she mightn't live to see the next spring.) / "Well, if *that* could be done M'sieur: it would be lovely!" (I had volunteered to take his latest photo with me. If — as was likely — they asked at the frisk=out? : surely I could carry a snapshot of my brother?!: "Nono; you can rely on it: I'll get it through. *And* deliver it!"). / "Naw — I take that back — not *that!*" (A snap of him boxing with a centaur; *and* a draw: "If it hadn't been for his beard damping my left-hooks to his chin: I could have knocked him out! — Oh they've got strength ok! But they lack our mobility: no legwork. But when they land a full-blooded straight one you really have got a job staying on your feet: they're not to be sneezed at!").

So, now we're on familiar ground: Didn't you, aren't you, do you happen to know? — He did, he had, he knew. / The things that

---

[34] Replaces the 'IRAS' (=International Republic for Artists and Scientists) of the original. I chose the name in revered memory of the — at least at one time — familiar play by the great Klopstock.

went on in these wall outposts: "In the past, when they were careless enough to think they could recruit green twelve to fifteen year-olds for guard duty." / Those times, some of them had climbed over the wall on moonlit nights: ". . . they've never been heard of again!" / Some had gone berserk, what with drill and desert loneliness; and mown down whole centaur herds with their MG! (So it's no wonder, any more, if they're slightly suspicious at the sight of foresters. And a bang often unleashes Panic Terror!) / "A boy once fell in love with a papillon! Gone quite crazy: spent all his free time with it; talked to it; slept with it at night; ran upstairs at every break — during rifle drill even — and in=deed!: it did look as if the creature showed some signs of attachment too! Never been observed before. Perched on his finger. Seems it learned to react to certain highly differentiated vowel sounds: when he shouted 'venez' — by golly, it came fluttering; we sat up in his room sometimes, watching." (So, he'd been a compatriot of Raoul's). / But the anecdote waxed gooeyly schmaltzy: how, after 3 months, the beloved mask became wrinkled; dessicated within 2 days; "sssshh'd" soundlessly for the last time — and then flattened itself, a rubber rag: the youth's tears; despair; *tentative de suicide;* loss of weight and other interesting symptoms. (By which time, mercifully, it had become a point of honour for all WACs: whether a cleancut girl could compete with a painted baby balloon?! With the hardly ignoble end result, that the crafty youth, quick as a whistle, managed to give each and every female aide that feeling of superiority which had been so dangerously threatened. (And his enraged superiors really gave him what for! He was then transferred for rehabilitation to an ocean radar station — *utterly* alone; one of those ten=by=ten platforms on 6 high iron stilts. Where he turned into a hopeless damned introvert.) — Y=yeah; that's how it happened.)

"*And this is* the Eureka Phare. — I'll drop you off at the Customs. — No; I've got to push on immediately to Portland." Cast a driver's allround glance, pulled a tense face (and played on almost all the knobs — : whoops, this one too!).

Shakehands by the custom house=wall; (the thick pinnacle of the lighthouse above us: just being switched off: for the sun was bursting through the roof of the giant silo, just as if another of those atomic reactors had exploded (all we need is the tuba, all-knowing and portentous of such local = last judgment!)). / : "Well, have a good trip Sergeant! And that I've delivered the goods — you'll soon see from your brother's next letter. — Nono, *I* thank *you:* Au revoir!". —

His place was already empty. I tucked the attaché case under my left arm (with the picture book: fucking paper — it weighed a goddam ton!), the match = bag right (which held the piece of mask = linen; tied round with blue silk ribbon, I'd observed!: "Geblüht im Sommerwinde, / gebleicht auf grüner Au', / ruht still es jetzt im Spinde, / als Stolz der Deutschen Frau!"[35]: that's the way my great=great=uncle would bitterly mock the launderings of his childhood — and no hominid-cloth then!).

Due to lack of a hand, gotta knock with your foot: at once one grey and one white–overalled mannikin opened, and admitted me right-away: "We've been expecting you." (*And* observing, I'll be bound). / More grey-and-whites joining in without delay: "We must hurry; the boat leaves in half an hour." : the greys got hold of my baggage; the whites leading me to a glass room the while.

"The examination was initially scheduled to take place aboard ship . . ." (whilst he held down my tongue with the spatula so's I couldn't squeak a dicky=bird. And he spied down my mouth (with such concentrated effort as if the hole were thirty yards deep: his right paw immediately groping for some kind of tonsil-clipper) . . .): "— but we've still got . . . right now

[35] An old-fashioned German washing-ditty.

we've got — enough — — : time!" (And synchronzing his last word with an emphatic dab of iodine on the uvula, giving me this humiliating hiccup: that's what these health merchants want!: that the poor sod of a patient, helplessly=vulgar has to burp away in front of 'em; to fart; say 'aaah' like an idiot; they make your legs kick smartly at their beck; they dressed modishly, oneself stripped defenceless!) / This joker pulled his paintbrush and spatula out of my gob with academic pride and joy, as if he'd achieved something notable=inimitable, his eyebrows raised saucily (and little hammers tapping all over me. Sucking cups of four stethoscopes on my back. An assistant tourniqué'd the band around my pulsing vein (so's my fingertips went all thick and red). Then of course I also had to lie down on the whitesheeted icecoldasusual leather couch. And while one (male or female?) twisted my genitals, another greedily counted my toes and fingers; the third pulled sample hairs from here, there and everywhere; another tugged lustily at my leg; I already felt myself pricked and penetrated in more body surfaces than I could count: Serum=Sera gushed into me.) / Then: "Sit up please!": A 'sister' appeared at the ready — (somehow there must be deep irony in this expression: but where?) — carrying a special syringe of repulsive length with a barbaric gleam in her eye: now they want my fluid, by way of return! (Feeling? — : like piercing a playing card. As they extracted spinal juice for a liquor diagnosis: "Just a tiny sample; you won't feel at all dizzy; the lumbar sac stays full." / The things I carry inside me: a lumbar sac!)

Dressed again; alone with the Chief Medic: "Tell me now — uh — otherwise everything's in order; we've given you injections to deal with minor damage; you're radioinactive: I'd recommend you visit a *dentist* sometime — yeah, what actually is that rash you've got on the glans? Harmless little blisters, certainly, we've analyzed the liquid content, but . . ." and he gave me an informationrequesting look:? / So I told him about my affair, 1 wanton girl, and the gay shenanigans with the clump of stinging nettles. / "Aha!" he sounded, satisfied, his mouth closed. Also nodded, as if to say that's what he'd thought all along. But wrinkled his brow nonetheless, just in case: and in point of fact I had to go back with him into the surgery; put it on a sterilized glassplate . . . till chemist and microscopist confirmed my testimony: "You will excuse us; but we have a duty after all . . ." (Big deal! — And at the end of the ceremony they unobtrusively gave me another shot: just in case).

Alone with my luggage once again, all of us sweetly smelling of hospital. / (What's the time?: "Hmmm: five-fifteen . . ." crooned the alto: I *should*'ve taken the matter-of-fact soprano!).

Up: and in the doorframe, navyblue and gold-edged, the captain himself. Medium height, straight as a rod, most reliably uniformed (living image of competence: even the crews of the ferryboats were — as is known through countless TV programmes — selected for their distinguished and photogenic qualities: the first step in the journey to perfection, into the land of the intellect and all ideals, 'Voyage de Zulma dans les pays des Fées').[36] / And I did feel an itch of excitement: it *was* quite a thing to be allowed in as a reporter! The first for about twelve years?: if I played this right, it could be a hecatomb: lolly=fame=&=joy, a long & healthy life! — I resolved to be at my best possible behaviour![37]

Along the quay, warehouses: "That's a very impressive complex!" (I; eagerly astounded. The other, brief): "Over 10 acres." / My cool=eliciting enquiries (I'm the guest-of-honour now without any doubt. And surely they'd think it 'unnatural' — even downright rude — if I were not to display the most impudent curiosity; always go a hair's breath beyond the

---

[36] A script with this title has not made itself known to me. Even French Histories of Literature contain no hint of its existence.

[37] As every serious reader (aware of the author's hereditary disposition: I'm thinking of his notorious great-great-uncle) will have hoped for anyway.

bounds of decency to cause shocked amusement; plus ingenuous boyish candour, fresh wind from Canada. Not at all superficial — give 'em a glimpse of a modicum of solid knowledge now and then — but nothing too profound: or the specialists (and the island population consists of the most specialized specialists, after all) bring out their unintelligibility = expertise kits. Play the part, stashing as much crucial gen as the notebook can take; *bon*. (Though I didn't trust myself: I was really too guileless and impulsive for these assignments! Had far too much devoted respect for Great Men, too; hypersensitivity towards works of art[38] — but deal with this here first.)

To wit, the warehouses: "Certainly. Mr Fitzsimmons can show you around; we've still got all of 8 minutes: this way please." / So was led through the nearest large sheds by the quicksilver Irishman: cases ("zinc-lined") of books from all countries (publishers must send 1 copy of each new publication. He pushed open the door to the packing room: aproned workers manhandling bundles of national and provincial newspapers.) / "Here's the urgent 'special mail': yes, it's going off with you. — Well, medicines and such. Ordered by the islanders. From Beltane to Samhain fresh fruit in freezers . . ."[39]: Urgent interruption on entering: "Mr Winer?:!" — and I pumped the redhead's paw updown: sure; they'd show me only what they wanted me to see! / And along the quay and over the gangplank.

On board: they introduced me to my personal '*official*' (to shadow me. Perhaps in fact to protect me so's I shouldn't fall down too many hatches: "2nd lieutenant Wilmington."). / Cranes heaving various steel drums aboard: "Liquid atomic fuel: to run our half of the island." (Didn't enhance the charms of this trip; my grey-tinted glance followed the ominously floating

---

[38] Compare the passages in question at a later stage: certainly one would have *wished* for such qualities in the author!
[39] Gaelic: 1 May to 31 October.

pillars). / "No. All ferryboats have exactly the same displacement. A thousand ton. The island harbours can't fit anything larger." :". . . *'harbours'*?: Plural?": "Definitely; two. — No: I'm not authorized to give you a map of the island." (Then softened this with a rider): "It wouldn't be any use to you anyway; we only have navigation charts which indicate the perimeter. But you'll definitely be given one there." (And if not, I'll ask for one; make a note right now).

Water bubbling all around the stern; in the hollow of my hand an iron wart (could feel another one with my fingertip): "We've got mighty powerful engines, capable of making 35 knots; average speed about 30." And to my logical follow-up query as to the duration of the journey: "Ohno, notatall: we'll be there in 12 hours *at the most:* the position has only just come through again." / He himself had never yet set foot there; just once spied it over the edge from a masthead. (So nothing noteworthy to be gleaned here then. — : "Is there any chance of lying down somewhere for an hour? I haven't had much kip over the last few nights." : I've seldom seen a man's face *quite* as relieved as 2nd Lieutenant Wilmington's! (Understandable: first, he had his duties to attend to; no one else was going to do his work for him, no one lifts a finger for him. And apart from that, a blithering observer was taking himself off — a civilian to boot: great!)).

But first to the loo again (and step back smartly after the pull: in a small-town hotel in Uruguay it had all flushed up on me once; I'm not the man that sort of thing happens to twice!). / And really, I was dog-tired: my bones felt wracked, jaw-muscles stretched. There was practically nothing to be seen aboard, on this little bucket (I could make up a stunning description of my crossing easily enough: my imagination is sufficiently intact (touch wood) to invent a trip on this tug! And grinned sadly, thinking of the hogwash I was gonna make my readers swallow: how I was pacing the planks charged with agitation — wasn't I about to come face to face with the Immortals?!

The most significant artists our generation had been kind enough to come up with? Virtually a trip towards Elysium; nothing but conversations with gods and heroes! — And my notes bound to prove enduring veracity qua historic documents, *'eternal' (unmovedmovingtogether)*[40] — and I quivered with another bout of melancholia: oh for a decent profession!).
— . — . — . —

Groaning, torso pushed up: mine: I don't want to dream any more!! / Got up and brushed my teeth fleet-of-hand (no, mustn't think of 'fleeting' or I'll start all that stuff again!: In my dream I'd walked into an empty country house. Instead of the barbaric antlers to be found sometimes, there were *human* heads on the walls of the passages!: you put your hat on them; you flung scarves 'round their neck stumps; between their teeth a ring with a hook and a hanger for your coat (and woe betide who dropped it! they got whacked at once so hard they rolled their eyes and boohoo rang out!). / A girl student came running and snapped her command: the red indicator of a tongue appeared in a man's face above, rolled slowly to the right corner of the mouth — while she pulled her stamp across; and let him lick it; then stuck it on the pink triangle of a billet-doux: it will make a holiday in hell, I dont wanna sleep no more!!).

A breeze across the deck; an 'Aah' from me (no, not released, no such thing; but a diversion): / And another yawn — What's the time then? : "Oh, that's not right, Mr Winer; your watch is wrong! You forgot to adjust for longitude: which do you use, Central or Eastern?" (Eastern. / And they'd eliminated 'Mountain'; the Hominid Zone runs through it; the few

---

[40] Quite apart from the misuse of the Goethe quote, this whole passage raises quite serious doubts about the credibility of the author, with regard to detail and adiaphora: he could quite easily have experienced the feelings of reverence etcetera, which he treated ironically, without giving anything of himself away. But — given the total lack of information from other quarters — one must make the best even of that sort of report.

border regions had adopted Central or Pacific time. / So I let my alto repeat her quick=tempo jabbering a few times . . .: done. / "And accordingly, time changes perpetually on the island too?". He only raised non-committal eyebrows: "Like any ship on the high seas, definitely. Which after all, it is." (He always said 'definitely' for 'yes', that one; I checked him out several times.)

"Oh, we entered the boundary zone long ago! 'IRAS' should be sighted any minute now."/The diameter measured about 380 nautical miles (or 660 versts)[41] and no strange vessel or aircraft was allowed in this sector too near the Holy of Holies! / Now the signal from the 'crow's nest' — and how pityingly he smiled at this purposely=pleasing landlubberish expression: Go on, feel superior! — : "In a quarter of an hour we'll see it from the fo'c'sle too."

On the fo'c'sle:? — *: !* / *: ??* : *!!!* : and then I too saw the deeper grey patch on the haze-strip of the horizon (and rightaway fold arms over flapping raincoat in a thoughtfully=moved way; visionary glance in that direction: Seeking the Grecian Homeland with the Soul[42] / He respected my silence for so long that I got bored.)

Ever closer: now a sailor constantly followed me with my baggage (and they grinned happily: Well, it's another world here, what? Mr Reporter=Sir; with 'laws of its own'?! — They'd be even more surprised at my report! If ever they get to see the original.)

It was within thirty degrees of my vision now and had turned ironblack; I could manage — though impeded by the roll of the deck — to make out towers, and high-rise buildings, with my pocket telescope. / "Trees as well?"; and he nodded confirmation: "Definitely."

---

[41] Equal to 700 old German kilometers.
[42] Paraphrase of Goethe quotation ('Iphigenia on Tauris') Tr.

"What are they doing along the side there?" : mannikins clung to what now resembled a wall; one slid down slowly (lower and lower; into the grey waters — and disappeared?!: "Frogmen: get rid of barnacles; renew paint." Crossed his arms tightly and oddly imperially compressed his mouth: "It's not easy work: the other day we fished out a dead one." / But deflected my questing look: "You'll find out for yourself. More than *we* know.").

The iron frontage gigantic now, our tiny ship gliding along it: not too close; for the waves were breaking with deep murmurings against the remorseless metal; slid upwards a bit; and sank back again, ashamed at the useless attempt: iron=bound! / A furious perpetual morse-din clattered from the radio operator's room; but although (as a newspaperman) I knew the form, I couldn't make any sense of it; probably all in code. —

"Now!": For our bow was turning irresistibly inward to the Iron Front. / Then I glimpsed a gap: a cleft!: an inlet it was, a good 100 yards wide! (On the right, palegreen huge lettering — lit up all night, probably) — :

IRAS
Starboard Harbour

Gliding through: betwixt canal-like banks: into a wide angular basin. / The water around us started to swirl, we were braking. Slower and slower. The deck was noticeably at an angle when we, with rudder and prŏpellor, got pressed onto the quay (where enough harbour crew were standing by ready to moor us unto the bollards. / Cranes arrived; turned with swaggering=stiff weightlifter arms, and slowly lowered their respective gear:!).

Why was he still holding me back with that hand movement?. His face bereft of expression; eyes aiming heaven-ward (full of white cloud ellipsoids, agreed — but . . . / : Oh-yeah, I see: the flagman on the bridge!)

Flagman on the bridge: all in navy blue, with wide bell-bottom-trousers. On top the ridiculous sailor hat, from whose rim fluttered *even* more childish streamers than normal. His arms stuck out stiffly on either side; elongated by little flags, white/red on the right side, black/yellow on the left. Bent forward, lurking . . .?

: and suddenly started to go fractionally berserk (that is, his arms!: Each of them became independent; snapping and flapping, each with its own madness; a semaphore seemed positively soulful by comparison. There! : another minute and they'd hectocotylize and swiftly fly away; each on its little flag — the one on the right up skywards, the other left down waterwards. / But Wilmington watched the wretched figure with such rigid satisfaction, as if he were surveying the ultimate achievement in human development unsnap before his very eyes. When the arms — against all expectation — stayed on after all, I asked indignantly: "What's the matter with him? Is it to do with my arrival?" "Definitely," he murmured wrinkling his brow: "He's signalling that the car containing

the welcoming committee is driving up; just stopping at the quay." — And just for *that* our man had to wave puppet=arms for a solid five minutes? And all poached on my valuable time?! After that I just couldn't resist the question: "Wouldn't it have been easier — speedier! — if he'd have *shouted* down?" / He looked at me, first as if I was a traitor; then an enemy; an idiot; finally a child: "But we are on board!". Making allowances because he was dealing with an island visitor. (And yet another of those puzzling reasons; noble simplicity, silent greatness. — Or is it really fraught with sense, only *I* don't get it . . .? — Then, much sobered, I ascended a so-called gangway: should I — to be pleasant — slip a 'definitely' into my parting words? But he was almost certainly immune to irony. / One could throw him a military salute at best with both hands at once, (*and* bow and smile silly = uneasily!: *that* combination would throw him utterly! — aah, forget it.))).

(But better 'proceed' slowly! Gain time; so's my head may rise dignified over the quay's edge. And I can see in my own time just *where* the welcoming committee's positioned itself . . . ? . . .: oh there; all's well.)

The Welcoming Committee: all 5 of them! : Brown and thin as a rake, an Arab sheikh; brown and gentle (and white-haired), an Indian. The black tailcoat belonged to the Chinaman: Keep Smiling. Straight and medium height (only: but, tremendously broad-shouldered and an ominous face to match): Comrade Uspenski. — Towering over them all by at least a head and half, my Yankee; casual, his hand in the trouser pocket of a summer suit.

The Indian stepped forward; looked at me with composed = cheerful dignity; the others pushed themselves behind him unceremoniously into a family portrait. (We were, I later found out, also televised and reported on from the lighthouse nearby: if I'd known *that,* I'd have left my coat with the luggage. Which the sailor had to carry after me anyway; as it was, it hung over my arm, idiotically!)

"Mister Winer? — : In the name of 'IRAS': We bid you welcome!". And passed me his skinny brown hand with a strangely wide (but free and beautiful) movement. (He keeps it brief. But good: at least he doesn't blab great chunks outa my 50-hour permit: *very* sensible!).

Then the rest of the colourful hands in a row: each man murmured his welcome. The Comrade was the only one to speak with normal volume (though it sounded much louder here): "Pogálovatj". My compatriot only grinned, gave me a Kentucky=handshake and casually shuffled behind us to the waiting minibus.

While we were starting (the Indian sat next to me; 'taking me over, is he'?): "Town Hall first. Where the Island's President will greet you: you must, of course, sign the 'Golden Book'!" (and smiled encouragingly: nice guy). / "Then we have 2 *quite* short lectures laid on, for your preliminary briefing, which is — as you'll be sure to agree later — necessary. For the rest of the day, it's still early, after all, we'll devise the programme together, to *your* taste: I dare say you've brought quite a number of wishes & queries with you; others will come up of their own accord."

Very slowly down 'Harbour Street': 30 yards wide (each lane 13; a pleasant strip of green in the middle, a carpet of chubby=cheeked flowers, colours married to scents. / And he pursed his little mouth in amusement: "No. The cars here *cannot* drive faster than 20 miles an hour: that's the way the engines are built. — Apart from ambulances of course; and the like." / Must note this 'and the like' down for questions later.)

"Two of these gentlemen, Mr Inglefield and Comrade Uspenski — will serve you in the respective uh=areas as guides." (Two female beskirted bicyclists floated past, on the other side. Also

glanced at us inquisitively. And once again, back over their bebloused shoulders.) / A long narrow little forest to the right (but very open: white air yonder was visible between the trunks here and there.) / A meadow and open country on the left (Faust & Mephisto roaring along on black steeds): in approximately — well, shall we say a third of a mile — a township began. My head was going backwards and forwards. I registered it all, and was all Argus as I rode along.

Halt?: Climb out: We'd hardly covered half a mile before turning into a small peaceful parking lot, lovely greenery (pleasant how medium-height thick-set trees accompany the streets and squares). / "Yes. In the 'strip' one only goes on foot."

Going on foot: we stepped through the tree scenery — , — , and stood facing an expanse of massive buildings extending to the far left and right! / : ? / "This here in front of us is the clinic — we're frail, and often and even gladly ill —" (smiled benevolently, wisdom of old age — or was it mischief? Couldn't figure it out right then). "Next door's the island's historical archive." We walked between both of them towards a building placed even more centrally, overshadowed by a narrow but very high tower: "Our Town Hall."

Up the cascading stairway; the portal a high arch — I couldn't take in more at the time; because, already waiting upstairs in his official shoulder-cape and broad shiny chain of office, the current President; Calistus Munbar. / (And bowing low for the handshake: the man was wearing red shoes! And ditto the councillors behind. — Straighten up again, all frank & open now. Letting one's eyes glow: at last, in the sanctuary of humanity: home at last!).

"Whallerá, whallerá; whalleráaa!"[43] : and opened his mouth gruesome wide (the throaty glottal nasal-roll of the early

---

[43] Another manifestation of the American journalistic rashness so alien to a European. In answer to a letter the author gave the following info — verbatim: it is 'constitutionally' impossible for him to take officialdom seriously.

Australians; I had to quite pull myself together to understand him?! — ? — (On the other hand, what could he possibly have to say? "Greetings" and "You'll know how to appreciate it", what?) So did my obeisance once again after the last Whallerá; and expressed, for my part, all the appropriate honours and pleasures, in careful accent-free Anglo-Saxon.[44] Another non-committal theatrical handshake; that's his Whallerá for him! / But now I can hardly go on behaving like a good little boy for much longer; let's hope we'll be moving on soonest!)).

On along under the looming barrel-vault, draughty, into the interior: the stairs were covered in deep pile runners. (From above, on the next floor up, an employee was about to ballerina down; braked — by digging the tip of her shoe into the carpet-moss, throwing her body back — and disappeared again immediately, silently, as before.)[45]

The 'Little Hall' was the venue for our 'welcome feast', eaten from a small side table (what I am saying, 'small side table'?: the massive mosaic top alone must have been worth ten thousand dollars!): a salt twiglet (some 'without' for the diet=freak), from a gold goblet, a tiny sip of Cape wine. (The thimble= glass — made of silver; embellished with the island coat of arms: the newly liberated Irish Harp[46] in a Zodiac made up of the initial letter of each of the contributing world powers — I was allowed to pocket it). / (The Russian, I observed through sheer coincidence, had slipped his uneaten salt-stick up his sleeve; and let the liquid slither swiftly into and out of his mouth!!). / All except the Indian excused themselves almost at once.

---

[44] ?

[45] In the margin of the original the author originally inserted 'pity' — later crossed out; as well as the description of the person in question.

[46] The painful frivolity of this formulation loses itself in face of its more earnest historical implications, though here as well, the author's casual attitude cannot be denied.

Round the huge rectangular writing-table (bronzed rogues with slipping trousers supported it at the corners):[47] there lay the "Golden Book" of the island; really more like a piece of furniture; in folio. On its own hand-carved mini writing-desk. / While he was opening the ink-well for me:

"*Tell me Mister Winer* — one question? : Just what is your connection with this old German writer, who was after all the first — even if it was just for a joke — to sketch the idea of the kind of island we have today: how are you related to him?" / So got out my documents and briefly branched out the family tree (he pretended to reject the papers indignantly; but nonetheless gave each one a searching glance!):

I, Charles Henry Winer, born 1978 in Bangor in the State of Maine. / My father: David Michael, born 1955. / His mother, Eve Kiesler, 1932. (And he nodded excitedly while counting it up). / : Her mother now, Lucy Schmidt, born 1911: "He was her brother, he was!" (Mutual father Friedrich Otto, born 1883).

"*I seeee*", he murmured, satisfied by many official stamps on the photocopies of the original documents (which I gave him as planned: the whole caboodle was after all no more than a milder form of passport control). / "So he *was* therefore according to this your=um . . .: greatgreatuncle." And I nodded with approbation: "My grandmother knew him personally. And told me umpteen anecdotes about him." (I cautiously did not volunteer their nature; most of them would have ended in 'fogging'. Hadn't exactly been a 'gentleman', my greatgreatuncle; perhaps fair=to=middling.). / "Ahwell; that'll interest our director of archives. As a matter of fact, he's working on an island chronicle; so the pre-history is particularly charming." —

---

[47] The author is referring to the famous archetypal group of 'Four Carpenters', especially created for this purpose by Don Pedro de Zapoteca y Rincon.

But now this "Golden Book": and he cleared his throat uneasily as I — all nonchalantly=thoughtful — began turning over the pages. ('Leaveoff, leaveoff, leaveoff!' was the message of his nervous fingerdrumming; but I wouldn't dream of doing so: what isn't explicitly forbidden me — and there'll be plenty of that! — is permitted). / And — wow! there were really quite a few things in it! for they'd perpetrated the blunder of decreeing that every resident or visitor on the island had to register *twice:* upon arrival on the upper half of his numbered page, on the lower on departure.

And lo and behold, one of the departing artists had given free vent to his feelings right there (and the contradiction between the respectful upper registration and the savage lower scrawl was a scream! Fiery affirmation above: "I am pleased . . . honour . . . total creativity . . . the good of mankind . . . pledge selflessly." Drunken scratchings below: "All a load of old crap: Yours Kilroy!") / Or here, the same sort of scene transposed into pretentiousness: Above: "This surely is the Promised Land . . .". Below: "Honest citizen: flee this land!". / His long-suffering sigh made me let him off the hook and I opened up the page allotted to me again. / "Well, yes; some are like young scamps." —

There! — And he nodded, pleased by my tidy handwriting. (I'd briefly and honestly set down as my motive: greatgreatuncle, and purpose: report on my visit. / "Yes, and so the day after tomorrow you'll have to — leave again, well. — I suggest: first of all you take a ride in the lift up to the tower with our town's master builder, so that you can obtain an overall first impression. You can finish there at any point and come down to see me in the statistics office: where it will be a pleasure for me to give you all the information you desire about our population and the like. — Agreed?" (Pressed a button under the tabletop. The town's master builder appeared instantly (he must've been waiting just behind the door); a little folder made of stiff cardboard under his angle-poise arm.) —

Just below the top of the tower was the narrow circular gallery: "Ahhh!" / . — . : !! / For the whole island lay below us like a relief map! A quick impatient tour round (no doubt something is bound to stick in my mind with eidectic precision); then back to him, who opened the folder, and held it — piqued — towards me: an exact map of the island, 3 inches representing 1 mile (so roughly = um, one to twenty thousand, good). / And all the while alternate looks across the panorama. He spoke in the customary mechanical touristguide-manner:

"*IRAS measures* exactly 3 miles from bow to stern;[48] its width is 1.7 . . ." — But I was quick to interrupt him (firstly on principle: I just *won't* let myself be bowled over by boring drivel! / And also I really did have questions, which were more important to me at the time than his decimals — a reef on which people usually like to ground themselves with great aplomb: I can measure all that myself from the map with a compass!).

"*So one hasn't been able,* as originally planned, to reproduce the measurements of the earth's axes to scale — in order to achieve the picture of a 'global village' right down to the last detail?" — : "No; that wouldn't have been possible, because the water resistance is immense; a slimmer line had to be chosen: the numerical eccentricity of the ellipsoid amounts to . . ." (and gabbled merrily on for some time, while I looked around intently: *your* eccentricity, too, I can unravel for myself later on! (*If* it should interest me at all))

In front and behind the double row of giant buildings. (He, just a shade more sensitive, after all, than I'd assumed, followed my glance; hopefully, was offended as well; hopefully, realized he should simply tell me *all* that *I* wanted to know: not a lecture

---

[48] 4827 meters according to old German measurement. From now on I shall translate in every case where it seems appropriate — i.e. with complicated, e.g., large numbers — into the metric system. (By which means the requisite codification will also simultaneously be achieved.)

my friend, but information — brief and to the point!). / So he did sullenly proceed to give me the names of the buildings I pointed to — "Everybody has his own way of learning how the land lies". — I inserted courteously; but he only pursed his lips in scorn (just keep on pursing!).

At the back: "*Firstly* the two libraries: yes indeed; right as well as left." / "Behind, also opposite each other: the Reynolds Gallery and the Pushkin Museum." / Winding up the view? : "The Theatre." (Then behind that the living quarters of the administrative staff — : "Where I'm sleeping tonight?". That's where he paid me off: "I don't know": Shut up! — / Finally 2 pylon giants sternward; for radio & television.).

Turned to the front: On the right the Hospital, Bank, Post-office. On the left (everything still in the direction of the great axis) the so-called 'smokeless industry': the island printing works, bookbindery, photographic studios: "And the like" (To hell with that expression!). / Then followed a sizeable wood, up to the two — yes, we might as well call them 'coasts'. And right at the front on the outer — ah well, call it 'bow': the terms 'ship' and 'island' keep merging in one's mind! — : "Observatory, Radar, Weather-station": Shut up!

"*So that is the street* I came up: from the harbour?" : "From *which* harbour?!" / Then I looked around even more bewildered: yes indeed: the thing had (as I'd already heard on the ferry-steamer) *two* harbours? And at last, of his own accord, he got round to talking about the basic division of the island.

"*Well, on both sides of the great axis*, 500 metres wide altogether, the socalled 'neutral strip'; with the administrative buildings, the communal museums" ('Andthelike'; yes, I know.) "Also neutral are the 'Wood of Solitude', 'Before the Gates'. Plus the airport and rocket-fields; although . . . quite right: over there. Beyond where my hand is pointing."

"The remainder of the starboard side takes in the Free World..."
— In answer to my hand spread out in amazement: "Ohyes, sorry; we say that amongst ourselves.": "Who is 'we'?" (but he avoided a reply, and explained further, mouthing faster):

"On the port side the Eastblockstates: there: the block of=nnum : skyscrapers." / "What do we call the giant thing with the dome on top?" I asked (so nonchalant and unemphatic, that he fell into the trap and bleated: "'The Kremlin'." But as soon as he saw me taking that down, he grew dead serious; and stiffly corrected himself: "The great department store of the port side.").

And a harbour for each side? : With its own warehouses, official-looking little houses, and its own lighthouse: greenish-white light on the right; on the left — most appropriate: it was port side, after all! — red light. / Was it so strictly divided?!

But of course! : "*Look* over there, the machine areas on both sides of the 'stern'? — Yes; 800 metres long, half as wide. — The power-propellors for the island are under Russian=uh care, on the left, USAmerican."

Each has its own vast sportsfield; each its parks and arable land. / The Americans had a charming little town (but with that confounded chessboard pattern!) erected for the artists: "Poets' Corner; yes." / The Russians had approximately a dozen huge skyscrapers (much broader; the fronts could well have been a hundred metres long!).

Hm. — — —

"*A few more questions*" I said: "After all the island consists of single steel chambers: how big; how many?" : Each 16 metres high; 10×10 on top. And about 123,000 of them; riveted together in five years. / "Its construction financed by whom?": "Originally on $1/_{100}$ of the armaments budget of the contributing countries: these within five years." / "That was the case in 1980 — as far as I can remember?". : "Yes; the island was completed then. In 2030 a new one will be built: precisely modelled on this old one here — at the most the propulsion will be made more up-to-date." (For a whole year mini-freighters carried nothing but soil. And humus; before everything was properly covered.)

The course?: was made public a month in advance. "We avoid storm areas when we can, and favour the Horse Latitudes: the Sargasso Sea & the calms. Right now we're steering towards the North Pacific here again." (The well-known one was in Mid-Atlantic. But there was also another smaller one South-East of New Zealand: calm and yellowy-green everywhere; waterplants, seaweed, neither currents nor cyclones; charming.)

"And I'm told you only call on quite specific free ports; in order to replenish provisions, andthelike?" / Yes=indeed: I myself got on in Eureka. For South America Valparaiso; for Africa Cape Town. For Russia, China, India and the surrounding conurbations, the Indian Port of Perth (formerly Australia). In these 4 depots all countries stored their artistic output and canned foods; everything, in fact, that was ordered. —

(And 1700 hours already!): "*Thanks!* I've had enough." (deliberately condescending: as befits one facing a bureaucrat.)[49]. / He restrained himself. And didn't even throw me off the platform. Instead, led me to the elevator. / Opened the elevator-door for me on the second floor: "The statistics office is on the right; round the corner. — No! Official duties call me away!". (And sank into the ground).

On red coconut matting (getting increasingly rougher: the further one got away from the reception rooms). (But hats off to them, the way they so calmly left me on my own: so I was at least able to look at the pictures on the walls without disturbance. (Viz., I might perhaps be under scrutiny after all, through some tiny

---

[49] sic!

peepholes: where on earth can one prevent that these days?!). /
All originals of course: no wonder, since the best painters sat
around here en masse! / A medallion here, from which a
bearded man looked at me amused: "Jules Verne"? — Never
heard of him![50] — (But he must have invented something
noteworthy, because at the bottom it said something about
"whose creative spirit"; MDCCC (and then on top of that a
string of figures just as long, XXVIII, ouch: how nice and easy
'1828' is to read; and how one has to fiddle around here!). Off
& on small sculptures. (Might be the inventor of the typewriter?: 1800-&-something sounded right.) / Here & there a
shorthand typist with elastic stride; Indian-style smoothly
parted hair; or another pitch=black with a face that looked as
if it had been designed for picking up meteors, not the kisses of
mortal men: I asked each and every one of them the way to the
statistics office, as they demurely tried to manoeuvre past me
(and each pointed to the same, ever nearing, oak-dark door-
posts: those chicks were just *too* delicious!).

Number Two, Five: Eight! : Twofiveeight, correct, so this is it:? /
"Come in!" — (Oh, I am disturbing you? : he had the vast
signature=folder in front of him; was reading and signing.
But instantly raised his hand while continuing to read: "Not at
all! I am — " (at this point turned over the page; the pencil
scanned the air faster) — "already. — . — . : Finished." Gave
the folder to a tarrying similarly sub-tropical beauty. Pushed
his chair back. Led me to the leather-chaired corner. — (And
legs crossed; notebook out!).).

"*Ask whatever you like.* — You were not previously acquainted
with the topography of the island at all, right?" : "Oh well,
who could know it?" I retorted: "At best the idiotic ashtrays in

---

[50] It was, of course, the contemporaneously well-known French popular writer; on whose 'Journey to the Centre of the Earth' our German writer Storm modelled his 'Regentrude' (Compare my Classics programme, Bonn 1966).

the shape of the isle, 'Greetings from IRAS'; and the friezes of Aguirre: nothing but Claude Lorrain plus William Turner! — The rest is room-furnishings with writers reading or having intellectual discussions; speed-painters in their studios; you know, whatever they think suitable for us to see on TV. — May I ask first of all about the population figures?" / (The card index was already providently placed under the table. He carefully lifted the dark-green solid=steel brick; opening it impressively (as if wondrous secrets were about to be revealed: what a fuss!) : then I saw many serious index cards, all apparently eager to answer me):

"*The population figures of IRAS* at this time amount to — : Five thousand and ninety-six." / Distribution: "Real artists & scientists 811." — "So ... approximately 1 genius for every 5 million people" I said heavily: "rather depressing, wouldn't you say? — Ohwell. — the others ...?". / The others all administrative staff: commercial, artisan and technical workers. — "What do you mean by 'artisan'?" (Commercial and technical was clear to me: for machines and offices,) — "Well, now" he said calmly, "shop keepers, postmen, dentists, cleaningwomen above all: Cooks. Andthelike." (And I nodded fatalistically: the world, the planet of the Andthelike.). / Ohyes, *that* was important: "May I know the distribution: men/women/children?" He breathed more deeply; but picked up the second index card and read out: "Children — we have fewest of those of course — 26 in all. Usually the children of higher officials. Men? : 2007. / The rest women." (Diplomatic; but I could figure it out after all: so there were more than 3000 women).

But then I had to soft-pedal: "May I know how many geniuses live on the starboard side?" — He didn't look at me, but said to his index card: "392 living geniuses on the right." / Joke question (to relieve the situation): "And how many deceased?" (and smile: must at all costs keep him in a good mood). He too grimaced wryly; acknowledged my naughtiness for a surprisingly long time; and finally answered: "Yes, we make some distinctions here." / Did the 'division' really extend to the *graveyards* then; and had I unwittingly touched on another sore point? For the subject made him suffer. — Change to something else, hopefully inoffensive!:

"The official languages?" : Indian, Chinese; American, Russian; Arabic, Spanish. / The newly-dead languages?: there was 1 Frenchman from Abidjan; 1 exiled Pole: "Of course, none of the original Germans survived; only those who happened to be travelling abroad: until a few years ago we employed 1 from the small, ever decreasing Argentine colony as a translator in the library. — But there are sufficient tape-recordings of all former European minor languages. / Yes, quite right: the core was made up of the teaching staff from the 'School for Design', which moved to Chubut in the nick of time. Yeah."

About the IRAS=prize: "Well, scholarships=or permanent residence on the island are awarded by a jury?" He massaged his Buddhist=thick earlobe thoughtfully; "Well", he said, hesitating: "That is=um — a ticklish point. Bound up with numerous difficulties. *And* complications. The procedure in a particular case is as follows:". / Each country was allocated free places to start with, according to the present quota of 1:5.000.000. And each put forward its candidates. — "But!" (and even he, the conciliate=neutral, raised his eyebrows sternly): "approximately three-quarters of these are, in practise, refused by our admissions committee! It is just *too* sad: in the mother countries, even political parties sometimes vindictively prevent the advancement of geniuses they find irksome. Or if the hero of a novel happens to bear the same name as a personal enemy of the chief critic — the author can be refused by him because of that! One has to know all that; and neutralize it: which is *very* difficult." (Mind you, once a country — "I don't want to mention any names" — had registered all its dissident writers, right down to the below average ones, for its quota of 53 free places. With the cunning motive : then they will be (a) removed (which also annoys the populace further : "Yes, they are trying to get to safety!"); and (b) after two years they're no longer competent to describe the subtle developments: no longer have 'their finger on the pulse of the nation': this, incidentally, is also the reason which all rejected candidates used to like giving to the press: a responsible artist shares the suffering & joy of 'his' people, they claimed!).

"*So, as a last resort, you* interposed your own admissions committee?". Yes. / And they were all experts and Great Old Men themselves, *very* careful; it would have been just too easy to make oneself look ridiculous for ever! They had more than learned their lesson when that fanatical American had turned down the Russian novel 'Sspihtshki'[51], to be the laughing stock of the entire civilized world. / The island commission could for its own part make suggestions, for which it took full responsibility: important for the unrecognized great; and also in case of an undeniable surfeit of geniuses in any one country: "So in the final analysis the purpose of the island *has* been fulfilled after all: objective selection; and definite promotion of great artists! Quite apart from the protection of important works of art." / It took quite some time before he said "Well... yes."

"*Ageing or burned-out geniuses?*": the Russians had pushed through the regulation that anyone who hadn't produced a noteworthy work of art within 2 years (or at least the promising beginnings of such a work) could be expelled again. / Yes, and furthermore: "Is there ever a case of an artist leaving the island of his own accord?": "Yeah well: ageing, or incapable or unwilling geniuses can theoretically be absorbed into the administration, as a privilege. Into the jury. or a position as a teacher, librarian" ('andthelike'?: no, this time he used): "andsuchlike, is provided for by the island's charter."

[51] The famous 'Matches' by Alexei Konstantinovitch Tshubinov (1939 — 2002).

Does that happen often?: I mean this business about going over into administration; or the voluntary leaving of the island?" — He swallowed; he turned his head, painful to watch; embarrassed, took out a card at random (blank: of course!). Muttered: "I don't have the exact figures — at the moment — — : um=two!" (I didn't want to make things difficult for the dear old boy, and good-naturedly took down the mini-figure (although I still didn't know what it stood for: voluntary leavers — had I perhaps stumbled, purely by chance, upon the two black sheep in the Golden Book?! Lucky, what?: A journalist *has* to be! — or were they those taken over into admin? Oh well, perhaps the issue will arise again later. Somehow or other.)).

Six Island Presidents alternating daily (they'd allowed me to be welcomed by the American, out of sheer courtesy), corresponding to to-day's super=powers: 1 Russian, 1 Chinese, 1 Indian; 1 Arab (for the whole of L'Afrique Noire), 1 Spaniard (South America); and of course my Calistus Munbar. (All decisions needed at least a two-thirds majority: the Americans found themselves, to their genuine surprise, nearly always outvoted!)

Care of the socalled 'halves' had been taken over by the two super-empires: the USAmericans to starboard; the Russians on the left (both also took responsibility for the power-engines etc: for the 'island' was a sort of 'twin=propelled steamer', with 2 independent locomotive-mechanisms, situated quite a long way out each side.)

Disagreements? : Oh dear!: and he immediately got the file from his desk: "The latest of this sort of thing: the port side has described the bells of the 2 tiny Western chapels as 'a peace-obstructing racket', which is said to prevent their people from carrying out serious work — 'inspiration-assassin' is what they call the innocently tolling verger; 'ideas-cosher', 'delicate-brain-wave rapist' — and they demand instantaneous cessation: 'should 25% of the earth's population — they mean the Christians — still be allowed to tyrannize the remaining 75%?!'". / "I see, and so what's to be done?". He pursed his lips blandly: "I would assume," he decided, "that in future they will transmit the noise into the homes of the interested parties by means of a tape-recording: one could also set up loudspeakers in the chapels, so that practically no sound will penetrate outside. — Mind you, it *really* was disturbing sometimes" he added confidentially. (Oh well, he was an Indian, after all.)

Visitors?: he read me the relevant paragraph from the island charter: / Occasional visitors — the permission for such visits as they occur being given by the Presidency — strangers, above all intellectuals, are allowed in for 50 hours at a time. But *never* politicians; professional soldiers, filmstars, boxing champs (of any weight); publishers, critics; persons who had been ordained in any religion . . . / Then talk about the subsequent precise definition of the rules. For instance, they had added the following postscript to 'professional soldiers': "or 'auxiliary services'; irrespective whether active or retired." — and then the argument had begun in earnest about the term 'auxiliary services'! / Next to the boxers they wrote 'and wrestlers' in the margin. / Rich gawkers, *very* rich ones, did have to be let in sometimes, alas; but they had to pay incredible sums into the 'promotion account'; (and only got to see certain things.)

"Can you imagine?! : In times of threatened warfare; when multimillionaires make desperate attempts to smuggle themselves into this our sanctuary, hallowed and respected by all parties: some have even come over disguised as *statues!*" (When the top half of Cooper was lifted off, to facilitate transport — a possibility which arose by chance: in fact the seam had been cleverly camouflaged by means of a broad hip-belt — they found the drugged widow of Horsemixer, the American newspaper-magnate, inside!). / But he was

obviously beginning to feel very uncomfortable. So I took my leave): "Today I would like to restrict myself — very systematically — to the Neutral Strip. After all, I'll be seeing the stern-side automatically later on, when I go to my hotel: *would* it be possible, therefore, to take a little trip for'ard, to the Observatory?". — (It *was* possible, of course. Apart from the chauffeur, an Indian came along, too, and the Arab from earlier on, from the quay: he still hadn't got any fatter.)[52]

In the open car: "*And please,* slowly, okay?" (Usually one was only allowed to *drive* in the Neutral Strip in very exceptional cases, in absolute emergencies: All the geniuses, even unto the greatest, had to go on foot. "Exercise does 'em a power of good", opined the Sheikh darkly, and pulled his haik closer round him. ("fat stay-at-homes" then?: had I misheard?!)

Like an enormous broad avenue. / : "No, that is the IRAS = Bank." (A solid building: the takings were, as is well-known, fabulous — on top of the state subsidies! : The monopoly for radio- and TV-channels with all the leading personalities! The endowments from title-hungry mining barons. The postage stamps; the products of the island printing works: "Over there, yes"). / A few businesses: stationers; carpenters (bookshelf-makers?); 'typewriter and calculator repair'. Corsetry; clothing, corsetry (sure: 3,000 women!). / A small hall?: "The fire-brigade. More to do than one would think," answered the mummy cold and wild: "Those guys are just *too* thoughtless!"

---

[52] What is the purpose of that sort of remark? Is it supposed to make the reader laugh? Or is the author trying to document his superiority? Or does he belong to that unfortunate class of people who laboriously achieve objectivity and free judgments only by continual acts of insolence (because they'd otherwise be at the mercy of every influence)? Or are there really human beings who are, as Winer characterizes them in an earlier book, "constitutionally disrespectful"? : But if the above remark actually did occur to our author on the spur of the moment, so that it was truly spontaneous, then this hypothesis, however incomprehensible, is hereby verified. In which case: it would seem that the man in question really was surprisingly, unusually and strikingly lean!

Isaywasn'tthat — : *Bense?: Sure it is:* the equestrian statue over there: "Couldn't we just stop for a minute?!". / (The titles of his works engraved on a pedestal. (Name and dates obviously.) The 'Young Talents' decidedly promoted by him behind. On the right, with glowing faces, his patrons and discoverers, gleefully pointing upwards, beaming "Well, what did I tell you!?" On the left, decoratively shackled, malicious critics, each with an asymmetrical gag in his envious mug: very tasteful! / "But why as an *equestrian?*!" The Indian explained:

Problems very soon arose around the monument issue. There was universal agreement that we had to have monuments. After lengthy and hard-hitting discussions a scale was eventually hit upon: the lowest would be a memorial tablet. Then, the next grade up, a relief: circular medallion with a head. Followed by a bust (erected as Herma). Then a life-size statue. Then sitting in a chair on a higher pedestal ("Like this one here — what'sisname?: Gerhart Hauptmann"?: "Quite right". / Wow, what finesse: he could lounge around here, while Alfred Döblin, next to him, had to stand on his feet: "You should have done that the other way round!" / They ignored my smart-alecky comment; we seemed to have stumbled on to the 'German Corner'). / So the equestrian statue was the top dog's pinnacle.

"*Since both halves of the island have to agree* to the erection of a monument there's usually a 'tit for tat'. — I.e., we neutrals wait until one is due from both sides, and then discreetly take in *both* suggestions. That's when the scale is operated: 2 memorial tablets for 1 relief: the rate is laid down." / And what if they discover later on that a memorial's been erected all too prematurely? Or if someone was over-rated earlier on, and then after decades it turns out that he was 'unworthy of the saddle'?: "The heads of all figures are removable; that can be altered again at any time." (I looked away apathetically for a long time: 'removable heads': *that* memory was about all I needed for my collection! Head-depots, head-cellars, bone-house, flying-heads, mask=linen ....). / "So what happens if they don't know what the genius in question looked like? Homer or Schnabel?". The solution was surprisingly simple: "I don't know." / And from now on we too had to go on foot.

Through the cemetery gate: the genius of the lowered torch cautioned us with his index finger on his mouth. The gravel crunched under our soles. (Important that: it was *prohibited* — and not just for technical reasons (vibrations occurred) — for more than ten people to walk in step at the same time anywhere on the island!). / Silence: a bird's hop-skip-and-jump. Above the lawn-sprinkler a man-sized cone-shaped fountain sprouted water-powder. A gardener measuring the beds with a green rod (wonder whether he uses a green hankie as well?[53]). Over James Joyce's grave the blackbird sat awaiting: Eleu loro: soft be his pillow. / ("They should have put up a whole *squadron* for him!" And we had to laugh, perforce — imagining the cavalcade: all along the profiles of Joyce — well, I mean to say!!).

In the crematorium: a small intimate mini-building. (Heat produced atomically: the corpse was pulverized in 3 minutes flat!). / And the cemetery-inspector, — meanwhile arriving — cautiously explained: the corpses of 'non-geniuses' were flown off, the 'others' buried here; cremated, mummified, as requested. "Or perhaps transported back to their homelands." / "How many?" He pulled the black notebook out of his black briefcase (no: hold on! : the inside was made of *white* leather: for Chinese burials); I'd asked him the number of cremations. — "Ah=m — : artists 0·4%, scientists 88.". (Extraordinary ratio; hardly any one of the real geniuses wanted to be burned: Too much imagination, presumably; so ultimately they're all still in some way superstitious. Apart from the said 0·4%.) / Meanwhile, back on the mainlands, they'd recognized that

---

[53] These sort of things really seem to pass through the author's mind indefatigably: even to such an otherwise irreproachable description, he has to append his piddling rider.

urn-cemeteries took up much less space: otherwise the dead would gradually dislodge the living. And propaganda was accordingly made: on one poster the deceased was depicted floating, smiling & totally phoenixed, up over the flames. On the other a disgraceful skeleton, all blood & slime, was ingeniously depicted with vile worms sneering revoltingly at the spectator. The Bible could drum up arguments for this — as indeed for anything?! — : Elijah & his Chariot of Fire![54]

Then we arrived — still on foot: out here behind the cemetery, in 'Solitude green' no vehicle was allowed except for genuine matters of life and death — in a beautiful wood (actually rather parklike, for the most part; an elderly couple played a silent game of badminton; a black poodle lay in the quaking-grass, and looked over to us; yip; you've gotta luvly yeller collar!).[55]

Chatting: I took it in as we were wandering along: own money (made of aluminium-bronze) minted as coins; not only so's the gentlemen didn't become *completely* inhuman and lose all sense of human misery; but above all because *everything just wasn't* entirely free for all. "That's what I'd thought till now!" : "Then you thought wrong" his arid voice replied. / Details: lodging was free. Food, laundry. A new typewriter every 2 years; paper & pencils as required. (But if a very la-di-da man could only write poetry on *hand-made* paper: *then* he had to pay for it out of his own pocket / Quite right: I wish I'd had

---

[54] I am well aware that well-meaning Protestant theologians in those times of change tended to reconcile their parishoners to cremation with this example — certainly a by no means contemptible instance of irenic spirit. Generally speaking, however, cremation cannot be justified from either Testament. (And much less so "anything", as the atheistic? — author insists on alleging.)

[55] Would it not have been better to present more important details instead of these scrupulous irrelevancies? In answer to this question the author wrote to me: "Apart from the fact that atmosphere, the milieu, are the most important thing in life, every responsible author will provide his own individuality be it found good or bad: so that the reader knows *the colour of the glass through which he has to see.*" — I won't argue the point.

wood-free paper all my life!). / Then there was another thing that was free, if he wasn't married, what I'll transcribe as 'Girl Friday' for which — after all, it was one of the most truly democratic creations of all time — this secretary had to give her OK. (Which they almost invariably did: they automatically shared the fame; and finally wrote themselves — usually a biography of their boss, in which the most thought-provoking innermost secrets came to light, yeswell.) — Must get them to give me a set of island money afterwards: the coins were real works of art. Could be handed to me at my departure, so that I wouldn't endanger the island budget. I stated my request to the Indian; and he promptly=obligingly rang it through from the Observatory.)

The Observatory (or more precisely: on top; on its observation-platform. — At first I had found one of the friendly gentlemen extremely arrogant; for, no matter what I said, asked, politely requested — : he just nodded civilly and produced a pensive "Mnyaya=ya." / Until I finally discovered the little button in his ear, and bawled at him from the right side: "Where are we at the moment!!" (To win him over: though I couldn't have cared less, I wrote down that we were on 138°16′ 24.2″ western longitude, and 40°16′ 58.4″ northern latitude: "16 minutes both times?!" — and he smiled blissfully: "Mnyaya=ya" : Now he was mine! — Average speed 8 nautical miles per hour, by the way.) / And a Schmidt-mirror with a 20 inch opening beneath the rotunda: these Schmidts!)

"What's cooking weather-wise tomorrow?" : in the Meteorological Institute next door; and he earnestly read out the latest bulletin for me; it was still brand new, just ruled off five minutes before. Right: "Tomorrow continues without rainfall. Clouding up towards dusk; wind coming up too. / Further forecast? : weather deterioration." "Ohwell, I'll soon know whether it's correct." : "It's correct!". / Precipitation by no means covered the demand for water; so there were supervaporisers and =distillers (with a concentration of fluoride, to

prevent tooth decay) over at the back in the two machine-areas. The bow-side walls of all buildings were stronger than the rest: gale protection, for when the island-head had to be pointed into the sudden squalls. They also had steel-walls fixed into the ground all around, which could be pushed up to break the wind. "We haven't had a storm for ages now: after all, we can choose." (Lucky country, that!).

Steps down to the sea?: "Only in the harbours. Everywhere else this strong high railing encircles the entire island." (At this a bony voice mumbled something about "drunken Giaurs", but the ill will was all too unmistakeable: if an artist is to create exceptional works, he's gotta put himself into a necessarily exceptional frame of mind; through what kinda stimuli, that's *his* affair entirely! / Whispering to the Indian: "What is *he* actually doing here?": the bleating Arab. And he, likewise: "Linguist: Scholarship in Coptic." (Ergo, a specialist in Egyptian darkness and similar ultra-important matters.)[56]

"*Is it still possible to view the library?* After all, it was already 1900 hours, and the sun was hugging the sea. (But they were open till 2000 hours. "Every day?": "Monday to Friday. Saturday, mornings only. Sundays on request."). / Back through the wood. The gardener was still measuring the beds in the cemetery. Then back again sternwise in an open convertible; felt like 'Fifth Avenue' (even had the appropriate number of 'beautiful people' there!). Round the town hall. / "And *which* library?" : "Who cares — : let's say the one on the left here!" (Which was in fact the 'right' one — according to the island coordinates.)

Doors & staircases as before: come on c'mon! (One walks too much through too many doors in life.)

[56] Coptic: the language of ancient Abyssinia, to which humanity — especially Church history — is indebted for many a wondrous discovery.

And, silently, into the reading-room — bound to be overcrowded: I didn't feel in the mood to be subjected to the reproachful=disturbed glares of 811 geniuses. (Or no, actually: divide by 2: because they had 2 libraries. — Nonetheless: I wouldn't put it past them to let me figure in their next book as a trampling trouble-maker! So just tread softly-softly on tip-toe!) . . .

. . . : ? . . . (hand on my chin) :

it was empty!! As if swept out!! — (Ohwell; it was late already. Suppertime, maybe.) / And I'd doubtless been announced: you just wait: I'll find you out yet!

Over to the lending section: "Could you . . ." (elderly; but with the most puissant charms, grey-satin sprayed, vinum pro sapientibus; not at all meagrely endowed, despite her 55 years. And I found myself embarked on involuntarily flirtatious smiling: ? — And she promptly leered back:! "Oh, *for that* I'll have to fetch the library director himself!". (A pair of thighs: the right flank Thusnelda, the left Messalina. And then, to top it all, the rear!!).).

The library director; who was genuinely touched: "To think that *this* should happen to me before I die!: Someone actually asks for Happel's 'The Insular Mandorell'?! — : Just *one* moment please . . ." / looked at my time-piece: 20 seconds (that sort of thing always interests newspaper-readers when it says: "Precisely 2 minutes & 20 seconds later it was placed in front of me!". And why not: then they can at least see that — some part, anyhow — of their taxes is not being squandered uselessly!). / Marvellous décor in that reading-room: polished desks of fine quality wood; comfortable armchairs in front of them: 40 seconds. Thousands of reference works along the walls; another gallery up aloft; ergo, twice as many again, at least 20,000!: 60. (Just then the director reappeared through a door: "Just coming: hang on!". / Mayaswell sound him out a bit: "Must be used a lot? I guess you're kept pretty busy?" He simply raised 2 averting hands: "Oh no, not really!" (Very polite, this man; though he must be waiting to knock off). But he hesitated; still had something on his mind: "You're the first for days, who . . ." / "The first? For days?" I asked, wrinkling my brow. And he looked round, embarrassed: The Arabsheikh nodded black & ominously at him, at once: Go on! Let him have it!

"The library is=*ah* — relatively little used. — Only by the scientists. But the literary gentlemen . . . at the moment we've only 4 regular patrons: 2 of these ask for prints from the Middle Ages now and then — with magic signs and so forth — and proceed to stare at them as if hypnotized for half an hour or more: maybe it's to strengthen their visual imagination; I don't know. / The third tries to=ah — steal miniature Elzevirs. / But the fourth — no! — one has to admit, he really works most meticulously! It's a *pleasure* to put out an 'Annuaire du Républicain' of 1793 for him; or to advise him: has a fine taste in literature, that gentleman!"

"Ah, here comes the 'Happel': there you are!" : 2 minutes 20 seconds! / Took the little old parchment-volume in both hands . . . (on the fly-leaf it said: 'Mister Richard Odoardo Grimer (1921–84) obtained this copy second-hand, at his own expense, and has placed it at the disposal of IRAS.' : another island-trick of raising money; pretty cunning. Or at least not stupid.) / So I leafed through the rare (?) item — ("No-no!: As far as I know there are only 5 copies left in existence. — Maybe a few more in private libraries", the librarian assured me) — regarding this tome my great-once-removed ancestor had written a one-hour radio programme a long time ago: no sloth he in cooking up pot-boiling jobs for himself! ("You speak German?" "Ja"; that was me) / Cimelia of inestimable worth. / And parish register extracts there in roughly 10 hours (typing telegraphists; nagging pastors' wives: "I say husband: the IRAS has rung up: Sign, sir — sign away, so's you can remain in the Church!")

Question (and it was a weighty one indeed; it really came right down to the meaning of the island!): "According to that the writers don't make use of this unique opportunity: of having all the books in the world at their disposal!? — : right?"

:Nothing: not at all!: "Those guys aren't accustomed to any kind of serious work at all!" / I, wrinkling my brow again: "Those *guys*?!". (But Ali Muhammed Ben Jussuf, Benwhat's'name, Ben=zine, Ben=Zole thereupon intervened: "*We* only call them 'those guys' between ourselves in day-to-day conversation.")

"*The writers?*" : "*Writers!*" — "The painters & musicians?": "Painters and musicians!" / And — after a swift reccy round the reading-room: nobody but us; also a Tieck=bust and the secretary (really, that woman's chassis: might have been built by the Romans!). — :

"*Most of them run completely to seed!* And are absolutely finished by the end of their 2 probationary years — the only thing that isn't finished is their one book! — Haven't done a stroke of work; geniuses at lazing around . . . and then they leave, and make *us* look bad!". / So they don't make use of the unsurpassed aids here?: "Absolutely not!: Anyone who sets foot in here is no longer considered a 'real writer' by them; presumably gets slandered too: a mere plagiarist. : If it depended on them our book-trade would go bankrupt!" / Weaklings (a knowing Valkyrian nod from the secretary): "booze as if they were the be-all and end-all of the Empire! Squander all their pocket-money on Alchozens . . ."[57] / "No: only the much maligned 'Mummified Minds' do well by us: they read, produce the finest stuff; are industrious; live quietly on their own . . ." he nodded, content with this paragon. / "But this is

---

[57] Arabic for a sheath-like 'over-coat'. And yet nothing — in my humble opinion — is more understandable than that an impoverished artist should seize the opportunity of suitably fitting himself out with new clothes: how low must he have sunk, who begrudges his highly-gifted fellow-citizen a protective coat!

terrible?! This means the whole point of the island would appear to..." Pause. Till our Son of the Desert, Secret of the Sahara, concluded my sentence with up=tight lips: "Complete failure." —

(With all these implements & aids!: Microfilms and desk-shaped projectors: one could effortlessly read the enlarged text on the DIN A 4 glass-frosted slide! Book orders were fulfilled by teleprinter within a matter of a few hours. All the antiquarian booksellers of the world sent their catalogues here first, so that the Parnassians could pick and choose for themselves as they pleased: "Futile: Not a soul! (always excepting the afore= mentioned paragon and the library administration) ever buys anything!"

"We are becoming more and more of a depot." — : "Well, that would be immensely important in itself" I said drearily. : "Yes—undoubtedly!" he confirmed happily; and, more confidentially, for the Happel had worked like magic): "Between ourselves: *I* have regarded that as our real purpose for *ages* now!". / What do you know!: any book one can possibly think of — many of which are no longer available for love or money across the rest of the world! — is there in 2 minutes 20 seconds: *And those guys don't avail themselves of the service!* (I was beginning to say 'those guys' myself!).

"So what's it like in the galleries?: aren't the painters busily copying there? Studying the techniques of the old masters?" — He just smiled mournfully; from the left, the right, up front. From behind like garlicky simoom emerged: "Only if one of them wants to steal a theme." (What a blasted toad!).

"But book thefts do occur": he nodded knowingly: "Like everywhere else. But we do know who has them. And parcels have to be vetted by customs first; packed under supervision: otherwise it would have been all up with the Gutenberg Bible or the small Rembrandts a long time ago." / And the in-

indispensable Neo=Destur=Formulation: "All those guys are 'criminal' in one way or another."

"No; the original manuscript section is unfortunately already closed. — By the way: 'Gottfried Bennet'!?: Do you mean *Gordon* Bennet; or Gottfried *Benn*?" (I'd really bungled there!: Nope, not Samuel Beckett either: "Just leave it, if it's closed already. I'll come round again some time.").

Here, this I just had to see! : "The partially — uh=mainly unpublished manuscript of your ancestor." / "But absolutely: since it's being given its first performance in the playhouse tonight — specially in your honour: What's wrong!" (Oh Gawd, that means I'll have to go to the theatre yet, later on. And I couldn't decipher the old man's antiquated scrawl either; just about managed the title: 'Massenbach Fights for Europe'. — I'd had no idea that anything like that even existed. — But I might have known that no one would have bid me here just for the colour of my pretty=blue eyes!"

"Well — sincere thanks: Truly: You have given me much to think about." (You can say that again: *I* wouldn't have minded working here without worries for a year! — Or were these librarians just lying? Exaggerated — and were offended, because not everyone came crawling every day asking for some god-awful old trash? So better hear the other side as well.). / They took me past the theatre, into the government section; to my hotel.

And, really, an attractive intimate boarding-house: 2 rooms and a bath! My luggage already there. / Wash — no; but must put on a fresh shirt. (Best spread out all my few things, otherwise I'll search myself bonkers; I could never find anything I'd lost. / Had already been given 2 books now. If you want to count the folder with the island-map as one of them.)

Lo and behold! In the pretty little mahogany box which I opened inquisitively, there on yellow velvet lay a complete set of island money. And in spite of my shortage of time I spent a few seconds on it: fantastic job! One needs a magnifying-glass to appreciate it properly. (The largest piece a 3 full inches in diameter, very light and hard. Tempered straw-yellow.) / But I had to tear myself away: Boy Oh boy, was I going to show off at home with these souvenirs! (If I — as could be expected — earned a lot from the serialization and subsequent book edition: they were bound to go like hot cakes; for sure! And then a little house; with a big library in it; 2, 3 original paintings on the walls . . .)

(After all, you'd have to have things like that: in that sort of a house!). —

And so far haven't seen a single famous person! ? Oh well, no doubt all the 'High Flyers'[58] would meet in the theatre.

Notebook in pocket: downstairs: quick, Charleshenry! . . .

"*Keep on straight ahead along the Centre Street?* No further than 100 Färsäk, can't miss it; ? : Thanks!" (And for now let's get moving fast in the direction indicated: let's hope his 'färsäks' aren't all that long![59] / (Half-left in the upper ether a very bright star?? — : Oh I see; the new Supernova with Lynx ascending. Further, the now generally accepted explanation for such Novae: that the inhabitants had set up too many atomic experiments, so that in this case it was a case of a perfectly natural stage in astral development.)

Here we are, can't miss it, indeed : The Theatron! / (In back of the open space, created by the two wings, Shakespeare's equestrian statue: my kingdom for a horse!). But then full speed ahead, round the outside, to the front, on towards the main entrance!).

---

[58] Clumsy translation of 'Haute Volée'.
[59] Färsäk, a Persian measure, fluctuating between 6,401 and 6,720 kilometers: the original 'parasange'. — In this case presumably used proverbially = jokingly by the information-dispenser to convey 'very near'.

A good hundred metres of palladian pillar parade (and up the characteristically uncomfortable steps; change my rhythm with every second step: the devil take all palaces!). / My Yankee from this morning was instantly detaching himself from one of the groups: "Hello, Mr Inglefield": "Hello!: Winer!" — And gave a gum-chewing explanation of the building. / There were 2 cinemas in the side-wings. Also a chamber music auditorium on the right, and a ballet theatre on the left. (A few little groups were already ambling unobtrusively towards us; and he chewed their names in my ear — indiscreet and loud: / The names!!: Now I could see them all with mine very own eyes! Tried to memorize details methodically: appearance, distinctive bearing, throat-clearing and spitting mannerisms: a flowing=grey longhair; the meditative blondilocks of an eminent septuagenarian; one over there who thrust his chin out dramatically; another leaned on the pillar next to him, arms folded gloomily: don't tell me they were still so vain?! Still desirous of being written about, praised, filmed, adored? (All that's understandable with someone who still has to make his name: the moneyed public, as is well-known, demands that no artist is allowed to resemble a human being. But this lot here were after all completely secure, financially as well as ideologically: one would sooner have expected them to give me, the nosey journalist, a kick in the pants!). My my, what 'apparitions'?! : One of them had grown himself a fox-red barbe à collier, and now — at 25 — already looked like a fully grown idiot! ("He's going off next spring", my guide confirmed.) A bean-pole of a sculptress with a straight black fringe hair-do and an unbelievably lean neck (round the base of which she wore a close-fitting thumb-thick ivory ring) came striding up to us; was Inglefield's girl-friend; and helped to explain. — "About time we went inside."

Through the foyer: splendid walk-ways; a cold buffet supper, which at that moment I'd have preferred to any play on our globe: a wine-god on the right, the goblet voluptuously tilted over his mouth. On the left, as counterpart, the 'Goddess of Good Food' grabbed sensuously at her marble smörgasbrod: one could see that it 'went to her figure'.

Interior decoration: chairs covered with red velvet in the stalls; only one balcony. / I was led by my two giant guardians through the usual labyrinthine paths to the box of honour (from which they immediately discreetly withdrew: "So that no one gets annoyed." — The glove-size of that sculptress! —).

Bong! — : *And gawped uncomprehendingly* down at all that display of top-boots, which my great-great-uncle had considered appropriate to make his 'Massenbach' comprehensible[60] : right from the first scene (in which the author turns into the hero); to the last, with lightning & thunder, in the forest of Bialokosh. / A few images not unimpressive for all that: the one of the nightcoach (with its vast wheels rotating in several directions: the mayors of the towns it 'drove through' in this way only ever appeared with half a torso, bowing and scraping up through the floor as if seen floatingly 'from above': quite cleverly done!). / And some prophetic=spicy comments from the 'little fat man' (that's how Massenbach was characterized in the programme) were striking enough. If he really *did* say before 1800 that "Europe will be a wilderness and America will take its place.": "Germany will be divided, just as Poland has been divided." (i.e., between the West and Russia: supposing he *really* did in fact say that even in those days . . .?!). / The Muscovite voices amongst them as well: "Anybody's welcome to say what I like!" : "Nobody lacks anything here that the others don't miss out on, too: thus we are all brothers." / But still: too many forgotten names. Too

---

[60] A tendentious glorification of the forgotten traitor of 1806; whose autobiography appeared with Brockhaus in 1809 — on which was based the unnecessarily detailed play (fortunately never printed in toto).

many confused scenes, 16 of them; one just couldn't make it out. (Just possibly, at best, by reading it; see whether they won't allow me a photocopy. — If it's not going to be too expensive.)

And at the buffet at last: all-out attack by the closed ranks of writers! Never have I seen people eat and drink with such energy; their jaws worked like castanets: the leonine head of a certain Theodor Däubler gazed on benevolently from the wall-relief. / I, too, flanked by my twin giants, succeeded in pushing my way through to the counter. Then laboriously, laden, back again to the calm regions alongside the red-nosed Goddess: a latter-day Aurora:

"Did you like it?": and I swayed my munching head indecisively — nnno; not really.; "How about you?"; he too moved his mug dismissively. : "Too much old-fashioned brass." / "And you? / : "I did", said the sculptress unexpectedly: "it gave me some good ideas — a 'Divided Europe'; each half rides off in a different direction: astride half of a stylized bull!:!!" — she choked; she pressed her plate into my hand; clenched her now free right hand in the ivory ring and whispered hastily — still interrupted by nervous-slight burping — bits of words: —, —, —, — !: "To the studio!" — And the erect-tall Eumenides stalked away, black through the crowds, her thinker's hand still dangling from her ring. "Oh, she is *soo* impulsive" — he confided in me, chewing; then added (his mouth full of caviar): "and really full of genius: what a woman!" / "No. I would like to meet particular poets, if possible, tomorrow — on their respective home ground. After all, they're predictably familiar just to look at." / But he took me all the way to the hotel: "I'll pick you up tomorrow morning: Bye-bye." —

Alone in the neutral hotel-room: roughly 2300 hours (leaving out the centimes): so it was just about time to try out the trick recommended by my old pal. On the 'phone . . ./ : "Yes, manager please?" — ; — ; "Winer here: today I . . . oh, you know? — Yeah: would it be possible for me — even tho' it's so late — to have a shorthand-typist for a few minutes? I just have a little bit I still ought to dictate . . ." / Who? Oh my god — whom should I quickly suggest? the plump one from the library perhaps? (Rather a heavy diet) Or . . . nono; better keep it very matter of fact=amazed: "Oh — whoever happens to be free at the moment: whatever causes *you* the least difficulties. — Yes, in the hotel here; the Government District Room: 33." / And full of anticipation. / Brief debate with my conscience the while: "Was it brazen?" : "Brazen for sure". Hmm — "But isn't it 'natural'?": " 'Natural' for sure". At least a little bit! Hmmh. — "But *mightn't* she confuse one's senses: this leather jerkin, crystal button, nott-pated, agate=ring, puke=stocking, caddis=garter, smooth=tongue . . ." : "For God's sake, Lord: whom meanst thou?!" — Now I had confused my conscience completely; it shut up dismayed; and I could happily go on contemplating the coins.)).

Ah! : Very softly 1 knock? — : So over I went and opened the door myself: an Indian girl in straw-yellow silk! (Small and dainty, yellow-brown; and with typewriter). Of that I gallantly relieved her; and placed it in the seating area on the little round table. / Begin business=like pro forma:

"*Yes; stamps as well.*" she confirmed; pulled out the whole sheet of 100: presented me with the tasteful little album of a complete series (all island buildings): "By order." (Mysterious way of expressing oneself. And clever: one becomes hellishly nosey! On whose authority might such a Lotus=maid give presents? Brahma or the head post-office?). The piercing emptiness of a glance. And bowed here glowing-black parting back over the keys. ("Well, dear conscience?!" — But that too only gave me the big eye, and belted up again, bewildered.). / So rushed through the addresses of my beloved relatives and acquaintances; the wording always the same stereo-typed: "Greetings: Charleshenry. / Greetings:

Charleshenry." / Two bundles of fingertwigs, peeled; a broad red bead topped each little tip. Experienced manoeuvres changed my tactics, dictating to this seven=times-wondrous creature upon the clean sheet thus: "The pale lily means awe: the lemon tree — impossibility; the violet vain hope — : the rose is you!"[61] — : ? — She lifted her head; reassessed; m; and smiled (though tired); and reflected. And nodded: Yes.

In the bra (inside the upper rim) a little pouch containing fragrant=faded herbs: up to her ankles she stood in the wine-red pool of the carpet. / I was already supine. / Grass-soft sizzling round her delicate=sooty feet when she came running up to me: my arms formed a sash for her. My mouth a brooch, which I stuck repeatedly on her breast.

Above me: her brow was now an expanse of cloud. / (Over her shoulder: the moon kept red-speckled time.) —

Pause. / *A gentle clear rumbling* rose from below her breastbone: she'd eaten too much sattapadavitihárena: sounded strangely and gandhara-like, resembling dark-green mulchy stems, monsoony salads, down the Indus, Iskander's passage, 'sattapadavitihárena': very good![62] Voice grown husky from nightdew; twenty lovelinesses lay here in confused disarray. / (Hadn't Thalia made a mistake after all? Rubbed me up with a more enticing type?: The church fathers had already maintained that God had made the upper half of man's body. Satan the lower: Team=work; Junction. / So — must bring Satan another small libation.)

She rinsed my sweat from the cleavage of her breasts: had had a future corpse as a covering (just as well we don't know exactly

---

[61] Source of quotation cannot be ascertained. (Maybe from one of the nonsensical encyclopaedias by that eternal 'great-great-uncle'?).
[62] Pali: curds.

how much we annoy and disgust women.[63] / I kissed her silently; and she withdrew, typewriter in paw.

Naked in front of the mirror: to whom was I indebted for such a gigantic jackpot, as a journalist, now and in the future?[64] : Virtually a complete stranger! : If I'd met that feller in the street, I wouldn't have recognized him! (Nor would my father). / Look down at my already slumbering frame: it's making the rounds, tormenting me. (Stop and think of something similar).

So brightly did the moon shine on my feet that I folded them. / Killed a gnat in my eye: with a bash of the lid. Often do that. (I didn't create the world! And if somebody some day wants to 'make me responsible', I'll strike him! (Of course, if he has 'the power', he can do so anyway; but I'll give him a piece of my mind!)). The slight vibration of the 'ground' becomes familiar very quickly; at first I'd had a feeling as though my legs were falling asleep all the time. / The moon immobile in the window; the red spot nearing the edge of the blackened part: when 50 years ago a young man dreamt of the mouths of his beloved, it would have been unexceptionable if the 'beloved' were many; if only one, then 'pornographic': what a blessing it is that those hypocritically=prudish Europeans have disappeared! 'Cradle of civilization' they always called themselves?: Well good luck to 'em! (And when one's grown-up one doesn't need a cradle any more: only this very evening Napoleon said that: *another* great man! / : Night-night.).

---

[63] The German reader should notice how after such performances — which in the New America, reputedly for being 'natural', have gotten into the habit of being freely engaged in — the inevitable backlash sets in: the Persians call it *Bidamag buden* (hangover).'

[64] Which has occurred quite often enough meanwhile, as is common knowledge. I shall be taking the opportunity again later of pointing out the divergencies between this submitted original and the universally familiar, very differently formulated, series of articles.

(And the whiskery all-over kiss of the camel-hair blanket: if only the next war would break out now! . . . .[65]. — . — . — . —

(Got up once: hands groping around in the over-ornamented room; feet assisting in the search: plumb-line of breath sound out . . . . . Ooooh. (I'd already started dreaming I was going to the loo and that I was disturbed by Griffin=Greifflings[66] every time I got to pushing: it's always high time by then!) And straight back into the multi-coloured checks!. . . . .).

The veil-dance of the curtains; the rest of the moon gone chalk-white: every morning one is transformed by means of chemicals, water & soap, from a greasy tousle-haired troll into a smooth-headed cool thinking being. / Straight down — I've no time to lose — into the breakfast room. — :

My Inglefield was already sitting there with a toothpick and Whiskysoda, to take delivery of me.

And he spoke / out of a smok / ed-up mouth: about the incomparable 'Starboard Chronicle' — he'd brought me the early edition: the 'Left Truth' which likewise appeared twice daily over there, just couldn't hold a candle to it! / While I wolfed down my lucullan feast: jellied crab; kipper-salad; I've always been a great lover of fish (have to stop right there again: how can you be a 'lover' of something you gobble up?! How imprecise our language still is!). — Liver-sausage with Swiss cheese on top. Blackcurrant juice. 6 eggs with slices of fried cheese. 1 steak. (And then some unholy mixture of macaroni & fried potatoes all tossed together with little bits of kidney, egg, and various types of grated cheeses. / He watched me casually:

---

[65] This passage was changed as follows for the articles, intended for public consumption: "Oh, if only all the world could share such joy with me!" Really, the repulsive egotism of the author knows no bounds.

[66] Meaning cannot be ascertained; the appropriate checkback was evaded.

there are some people, after all, who can eat a radish without having to think of Andreas Hartkopf (hard-of-head!).⁶⁷

"Island police?": he'd used the expression, and I made enquiries. / Difficult job, taming pissed poets! "A person who smashes windows at night and habitually gets into brawls is removed from the island." (But very wholesome rules: box a person's ears and you get one back. And as the cops were usually 2 metres high, and the poets 1.65 on average, that was *very* instructive for the unruly wordsmiths: they were, after all, here to *work*, not to play the bigshot: "*Quite* right. Mister Inglefield.").

But each obviously slandered the other: you just couldn't talk to Inglefield about port-side! (As if it wasn't enough that the nations outside were feuding: do we have to have that here as well?!). / Thus cold-bloodedly interrupted him; and communicated my list:

"*I still want* to go to the work-shop to see Mercier the painter." — He nodded, showing lots of lower lip; we should be able to manage that. / "Then over to Bob Singleton." (The notorious prose writer and freethinker. And he was visibly alarmed: would have to ring up first for that! "A great man, no doubt about it." But had been throwing everyone out for years; always with the same excuse: new novella. — "Well, I'll try.")/ And finally Humphrey Seneca Groatsworth. But he shook his head dubiously: "I think he's still asleep. — However, not a hundred percent sure." : "Asleep?" (I, uncomprehending). (What an inane excuse: if he's still asleep at 10, we'll just try again at 11!): "After all — he must wake up some time!" — "I hope so", said the unflappable creature before me. ("Maybe not either" he mumbled as a follow-up? Davus sum, non Oedipus!).

Stand up. (My luggage was immediately taken along by an athletic youth, and docked at the American controlled

---

⁶⁷ 'Andreas Hartkopf': 18th century German novella; *I* couldn't get hold of it — *I* hadn't been on the island.

starboard-hotel, where I was supposed to have lunch.) "I'll just very briefly show you our Machine Quarter."

The vast naked area?: Approximately 1 kilometre long, half as wide? — And he nodded: "Right". / Only one single building was anchored on the iron-sea (for at this point the floor of the island lay uncovered and waffle=cast at our feet. I trembled within: that's what it had looked like in the desolate suburbs, between whose frighteningly isolated housecrags I'd been raised!). "The water-works". (Where sea water was boiled and distilled. We approached a windowless part; and climbed downwards through a manhole.)

Below: at first I saw only a wheel of terrifying height. / Pounding in the lubricated darkness: so regularly!) A face joined us; and regarded me scornfully through the wire-meshing of his eyebrows. (Because I still couldn't see: the oil can had to be removed charitably from my dead-end track.)

"Atomic combustion?" (I'd already heard about it on the ferry; but): "didn't they originally say that was to be absolutely forbidden on the island? To bring in atomic power?" The head engineer only wrinkled his right cheek to a non=laugh. "D'you really think the Bolshies[68] stuck to that? — Once we noticed that a Russian woman who often travelled back and forth as a courier was wearing those extraordinarily enormous ear-rings: we pursued her straight away with the Geiger Counter :?:!!". — And even the head engineer nodded grimly: No need for false modesty with regard to the 'Good Atoms'![69]

---

[68] Slang for 'Bolsheviks'.
[69] In reference to the famous book 'The Good Atoms' by Thomas L. Fox, which promised 1 year before the outbreak of war, with irresistible technical optimism, that everyone would get a one-family house surrounded by undulating bushes and healthy dancing two-legged children. — The author had been bought — as was discovered after the war — by all the then extant 'Western Powers' (due to whose influence an island-grant had also been obtained for him, so that he survived).

(And the things the Russians were supposed to be getting up to over there!: Only employed 'safe' people as responsible technicians. I, sceptically: "Is there really such a thing?" And he "Why yes!: Apparently they have a colony in Siberia — far away from any other humans — where they speak only one language, specifically invented for this purpose. With a very small special vocabulary which the ordinary Russian can't even understand. Only marry amongst themselves. Never give anything away. Absolutely spy-drug-proof: we've tried them! Haven't got names for many things: when we inquired as to the state of Russian atomic experiments, this hypnotic guy got up, folded his arms over his chest and did a sort of Cossack dance." "How many atom bombs have you got here on the island?": same result; but there must have been quite a few, because he flapped about for a good thirty seconds! "Yeah=yeah — things look pretty different over here in the Free World, what?" — I looked around me: is that the impression I was getting? (And how *about* that for super-cerebral finesse! — Even if it should turn out *not* to be true!).).

"Oh but of course we'll drive!": he swung behind the wheel of a mini-Cadillac; and we glided back through the Iron Gate. ("Kekulé?" the sentry had asked; and got "Wyer Street" in reply. And something else in whispers.) / "Beautiful playing fields!". But not used much; only a couple of slim WACs hoisting themselves on gymnasts' rings — tilting, rotating and spreading their legs apart: "And the Poets?". But he calmly repudiated: "A Poet doesn't run."; and parked slowly just outside the town.

First of all the 'Serpentine': "Beautiful!" The murmuring water swished down from the Poulaphouca River, round and round the hedge. ("Oparoke", "Oparoke", croaked a few veritable frogs in the still of the morn); from the little bridge, over which slooped a weeping-willowtree, the Poets' Corner looked wonderfully sleepy: "Charming!". / Chessboard plan: seemed as though the white squares were gardens; the black ones occupied by a one-family house at each corner?: "Exactly so." / How many houses did the area boast at that time?: "67".— "*And* the department store: over there." —

Through the still deserted streets: mind you, it was only half past eight, and artists sleep late. But he shook his head sceptically: "*Lazy* artists, yes." / On the contrary, the industrious ones got up at 4 in the morning to take advantage of the precious peace for their work; and then by 10, when the others were twisting their yawning bodies to light, they were admittedly tired again, but they'd achieved something. — "And this happens often?" "The lazy ones?: Yes." (Actually I'd meant it the other way round; but the information was just as satisfactory that-a-way too.)

Streets named after — '*dead!*' — *artists:* 'Coleridge Road'; 'Keats' Drive'; 'Brontë Square' (And there they were, the Sisters Three, reading & writing: Charlotte, straight-erect, right breast in her own hand (so that, quite cleverly, it swelled slightly through the distended fingers: searching for the land of love with her soul. / Emily seated with wrinkled brow, her bronze heel moulded deep down into the bronze pedestal. / (Finally Anne; very shy and childlike; a quill-pen pressed to her lips). / : "Lovely!".)

Pets?: Were permitted: Monkeys, dogs, cats, singing birds. seawater-aquariums. (All of course carefully checked, disinfected and the like before importation.) / Free-ranging wildlife: crows, hares, lizards; moles. / Domestic animals out in the 'fields & pastures': horses, cattle; pigs, sheep; goats, hens, ducks.

Beautiful plants: Youngpoplars with ravishing figures! I loved to stop in front of the little garden: 2 shrubby treelets were shyly holding hands, a red beech and a double-leafed maple: "Looks very nice!". And he nodded philosophically: "The gardeners are right on the ball".

Apart from which — and he coolly rummaged in his pocket — 'my Mercier' lived just here. (In the neighbouring house someone who knew how was just beginning to belabour his piano with pretty barbaric virtuosity). Inglefield shrugged his shoulders thoughtfully; but then, as I wouldn't leave off, said greasily: "Try him." / And I rang in spite of his warning about the unsociable fellow (also unobtrusively took something out of my wallet).

The door flew open: he was raising his palette ready to clout whomsoever round the earhole! But with admirable control (for an artist) he tore the brush-bouquet from his mouth with his right hand and bawled: "I've no time to show pictures!!" / So quick-as-a-flash I bawled back: "But perhaps to look at one?!" and synchronized by pushing his brother's picture under his nose. / (He had to collect himself first. Had come as too much of a surprise. But gradually he started to smile. — "Très bien." he growled aggreeably. And: "Come inside with me."). / Inglefield, tactfully, bade permission to use the telephone: wanted to inquire how far his sweetheart had got with the bisected Europa.)

"*You have seen mon très cher frère?!*" : so report very briefly and to the point, the most casual acquaintance; but he was very pleased all the same: "I haven't seen him for 2 years: he's become a Sergeant?": "And how!" I replied (and he *had* been a splendid specimen, that tall Canadian!). / But:

"*No! : I must move on:* I'm allowed in for 50 hours as a journalist; of which — oh, my God — 18 have already gone: really, *I've* nothing further to relate; and *you* are in the middle of your work; I only wanted to keep my promise!" Shook his least-painted elbow. And then, in the wake of Inglefield, into the posh residential quarter.

"*But the interior décor was very grand!*" : "You may well say so: they have everything here that their hearts desire, these writers! : Three hot meals a day; and any number of cold ones they want. A new suit every year; every-day clothes made to measure on request. On doctor's permission, free nescafé: on doctor's prescription, low-pressure air conditioning installed in their studies — there you go!" / "Well" I mused; "1 suit a year — : that's not really all *that* much . . . ." But he wised me up further:! / And, indeed: when you took *that* into consideration, 'those guys' wouldn't really have needed even this perk. For: "You can't imagine how the largest firms compete to be allowed to supply us *gratis!* Just so they can later advertise: "What does one wear on IRAS?: Eagle=shoes! — : Could *you* resist a television ad in which Frederick Nelson rears his snowy mane, vigorously pounds the keyboard with his right hand and proclaims — '1 drama more a year with Remington!?' / (Quite true; after all I myself had once used dextrose for months: just because the white gods here allegedly enjoyed nothing — or at least very little — else; unless it be Bigtails Wheatgerm-oil.) / "Can you imagine the sort of parcels most of them send home: whole *bundles* of clothing!"

And the furniture as well?: Yes, everything, everything free! — Even the giant Fono=Vision=Cabinet? : That too. / Beds of truly unchristian bounciness. Secretaries at one's beck and call at any hour, day or night, for dictation: "If you didn't write poetry before, you'd start here . . . . that's what we thought." —

From time to time the poets got that well-known bee in their bonnets about 'the simple life': a log-cabin was immediately placed at their disposal on the Otsego=Lake. : "Would it be possible for me to see something like that?!" (Would make an article in itself! Just the right thing for those revered Abderites![70] — But that would mean calling one of the 'solitaries' first; and so we drove to his girlfriend's) — :

---

[70] Remarkable the candour (I choose a mild expression) with which the author derides the middle-class section of his public like that: especially if you consider the fact that he doesn't disdain his salary, which depends upon the selfsame despised good-natured credulity.

who today was all white, paste-powdered!: opened up for us, absent-minded limbs; didn't recognize us; just possibly Inglefield's voice; but then embraced me by mistake (and her brand of plaster of Paris tasted revolting!). Then stumbled, ahead of us, hither=and=dithering between negro-sculptures and Sardinian stuff (on which most of the modern artists 'fortify their vision'); into the studio —

: ? ; ! ———— : What the devil : that really was something! / The bull full-bodiedly ball=buffaloed — all Altamira and lecherous red sneer (and the quivering tool, like a soldier who hasn't had home-leave for 22 months; I speak from experience). A second black bull was growing out of his shadow — cunningly imitating the latter, extending the shape and using it for his own outline: but slimmer, venomously=suppler, with more craftily=curving horns. / And straddling each of them 'his own' Europa: stiff and thin and precious=grey in front: sinuous, thin, liquorice=sticky behind! (So that's what Miss Sutton looked like naked; hadn't had another model in that much of a hurry. Or maybe hadn't wanted one: poor Inglefield!). / (But now for an intellectually brilliant utterance. — And just keep on murmuring ecstatically till I think of something; marvelling & moving round...)

Ha; Yip; here it comes!: "*You're a* Manichean!!" (With the roaring intonation of supremely enchanted admiration — and indeed it *was* a helluvah inspiration from that girl!)

She stood there, her body grey all over; stone-jaws clapped open a few times — then she shouted for joy, cricket-soft yet with chiselsharp strength: "Oh really! That's me!". (And in unison we expounded the necessary pairs of concepts to the eager Inglefield: Ormuzd & Ahriman; Day & Night; Starboard & Portside. / Then I surpassed myself with the even more elegant phrase 'Black & White'. She embraced me again, yet again did I feel the grating of her ribs. And together we got the thus happily evoked whisky-bottle from the ingeniously=untidied kitchen.) Inglefield just sipped, and then worriedly clambered up to the upper floor to phone.

Alone with the pale see-through vertebrate: who was completely muddled ('spent' from the exertions of her hard day's night; ex=hausted; and now the 2 tumblers-full of hooch on top of that!); arms going like scarecrows; we leapt up to encircle the new group once again: the gusto of the black partners was magnificent!: "A dangerous turning-point: Black is just coming in: Cave!" : "Quite so: it is a success." she said happily. And again hung her arms from above onto my shoulders (instinct of the pooped: Hold on! My nose just about reached up to her chest; and, out of purely scientific interest, I gave it a quick good feel — ? — : no : not a trace. In back one could quite effortlessly take her spine in one's hand, like a knobbled stick. Waist measurements? — Well, about 60 centimetres (and that at 2 meters 12 height: poor Inglefield!). / Worn-out she subsided on the broad-leather daybed. Wanted another drink; but I held my hand over it forcefully, and she thanked me in high C for my concern: "You are right: I ought to be looked after all the time.") / Inglefield's treads downward; he seemed relieved:

"*Alright. We can* go and see both of them. — In a quarter of an hour: so I'll just briefly show you our harbour and airport beforehand. — Bertie? : Good bye. And get some sleep now." / He then carefully wrapped 2 blankets round her (one alone would have been too short) — : then the wan=bony face really looked like a little nutcracker out of the garish plaids. The mouth was still open, practising weird whispers; accompanied by eye-gawps. (But soon calm descended, as if covered by a spider's web; the features smoothed themselves out. The first deep breath. We stood back delicately. And again. — Then a shrill voice said, with bone-whistling energy: "The foot! — The foot of the blackwench: must be *smaller!*" / Snug sigh, like a retreating wind whistling through railings. Then a turnabout, 1000 limbs stirring simultaneously... And we tiptoed, nodding at each other knowingly, through various doors: "What a woman!").

Up Harbour Street: "*Over there,* behind the trees, the hotel: where we'll have lunch later on." / "Not too much of the harbour" I pleaded, "because I already took quite good note of it when I arrived; there are more interesting things hereabouts." (But still had to go along, at least into one of the warehouses where provisions were stored. : "D'you think I could have a can opened for me?". / He just smiled at my suspicions; and I was allowed to choose whatever I liked. — "Let's say=uh — , — : here; this one!". ('Quality calves'-liver-sausage' — I had in fact suddenly become hungry, and had inhibitions about demanding provender yet again!). / So I sampled it, with critically=wrinkled brow; again and again, with a table-spoon: all the way down to the spicy jelly-base — three-quarters of a pound, no bones. (And they watched: confident at first. Then less sure, as I went down further. Halfway down the can, amused. Then perplexed = questioning. Deep thought=burrows. And nodded at the sound of the spoon carefully scratching the base at last, in dazed mutual approval: doesn't stint himself, this guy! : There's no having him on! (And raised their hands proudly when I liver-sausagely proclaimed: "Faultless!" (which fact I also immediately put down in writing with an earnest expression): Let the eagle scream!). / Unobtrusively widen my belt 2 holes.)).

Here's the airport: USAmerican personnel bustling about the runway (though it was officially neutral ground!): "We had to give up the rocket-base to the Bolshies for it." / Right: some of them were creeping around over there. / Or rather no: must be correct!: They were by no means 'creeping'; they *walked* rather, squat and self-assured, a fully grown screwdriver in each hand. / And farther away, back up a stretch of 'Harbour Street' again, round many confusing bends (some of them unnecessary?: or so it almost seemed on my map. / One never had the feeling of being on a sort of ship!). —

A visit to the modern hermit: "I want to be a loner." he'd informed the island management 8 days before, gloomy & monosyllabic; and had moved to the country. / A rough, arty longfibred =scruffy suit looked very good on him. (Telephone; in the entrance hall. I tried out his lavatory straight away: snazzy bog-roll!: 2 ply; firm and handy on the outside; inside satiny and soft: : 'Your family will be impressed — your guests will rave about it', 'ultimate absorption'. And after 4 weeks when it had been island-tested, some quite different things would be printed on it; mustn't let myself think about that!). / Charming, the bitter rudeness with which he played the host. Also had the most delightful array of misanthropic phrases at the ready and forbore to spare us any of them — indeed he was kind enough to repeat one which, on account of its length, I hadn't cottoned onto at first so that I could preserve it in writing. / (But the vitality of the man was something else! : After all, he must have been well over 80 — yes of course: wasn't he born in 1921? — and still had not a *single* white hair; nor a missing tooth; and had a secretary laid on for half past ten? — Ohwell; they just didn't have any problems here. And artists have cast-iron gonads anyhow: hadn't Titian live to be 100 and still at it? and Fontenelle even the 'Secretaire perpetuel'. / He nevertheless seemed strangely pleased about our visit (although he regaled us with ever=ready hermit-esque idiocies re the 'disturbance'. We came on oh *ever=so* guiltily=awestruck!). / Basically a charming old man after all. And his books — *when* he did write any — weren't at all bad. Though not in my line; but that's not saying anything. / Right on time the secretary rescued us: and we were pushed, with genial boorishness, towards the door; one more thundering nod — (and then ostentatiously locked it:!).

"Yes; exactly so." (Inglefield, lethargically): "He'll be back in town in 8 days at the outside." / But there were also those who

always lived 'beyond the gates': "They are *very* highly regarded.": Quiet industrious types. Just come in every 4 to 5 days to shop, avail themselves thoroughly of the book-treasures; and deliver their script on time: "Like your man Bob Singleton to whom we're driving now." / And he was the one I was really eager to meet — the notorious atheist and radical!

Hang on; one more thing: "He has preserved himself remarkably well, that Hermit just now: he must have a good 87 years on his back, and that's a modest estimate!" / His eyes sparkled behind his cornea; he giggled grandly through his nose; he seemed to become a secretive=stranger: "Yes. — And no." — he confided to the steering-wheel. (Until I was bewildered. But yet it seemed uncalled-for and unhelpfully=subtle?: 'Yes', that meant he was 87. 'No': he had preserved himself well: subject closed; what the hell?).

Through 'Fields & Pastures':[71] The nutritive bustle of the farmers working the fields: they scratch and neigh, scratch and neigh, scratch and neigh: a watchmaker could have made a better job of them! (A cattle-yoke: the black ox with the white cravat had something *clerical* about him; the athletic shrew behind, a rag knotted around her bulky pate, the careless awning of a dress: 99 cents in the dollar are always missing as far as I'm concerned when I hear country folk glorified as 'the backbone of the nation' or similar clap-trap.) / Explanation: they were there not merely to enliven the landscape (adjuncts); but also for potato and grain production, in case of extreme emergency. Fields were shone upon, rain could be laid on; stabling for the cattle: and this 'peasantry' had twice already had the nerve to demand "its share in the island management". Each time they were summarily banished from the island; but the last time the ringleader — a Russian, as they

---

[71] The following peroration merely documents this lumpen= reporter's lack of contact with agriculture; and is only informative insofar as it reveals a further limitation of the author.

subsequently discovered on autopsy — had had to be shot: "Instead of being overjoyed that they are permitted to live here free from war!" / Truly: there are no limits to the insolence of these clodhoppers! : all over the world they prevent the importation of cheap foodstuff: if they can't produce it as cheaply let 'em look for another job! / On principle always vote chauvinistically right-wing — which is closely allied to the fact that it's they, of course, who always make the 'best soldiers': i.e., *'those* oxen who choose the butcher for their king'!"[72] / Inglefield nodded at such opinions; but nonetheless immediately qualified them, shoulder-shrugging: "We need them." — To which I protested heatedly: "Haven't the Russians and Chinese transformed theirs with the greatest success into 'Workers of the Field'? Where food is produced by the purest factory methods on the grand scale?: Surely it is *precisely* this conception which enables their products to be at least a third cheaper than ours: so why don't we get rid of the hypocritical stable-muck halo around these rogues *too;* all that mystical mucky hoo=hah about 'Blood & Soil' . . ." / But he cut me short; quietly and urgently, in a way that I hadn't heard him speak before:

"Mister Winer: a word of advice: Beware of admiring the Russians: that could land you in a whole lot of trouble! — I've received instructions — I have — I don't want to say 'officially'; but almost that — I have to advise you against an overly extended visit to the port side. Above all, you should on no account — you'd presumably originally intended to — spend your *last* day there of all things. And make sure you don't leave by Sovrop."[73] (and again more calmly-flattering): "Why don't you spend your last hours with us tomorrow?: we

---

[72] Quote from the likewise anti-military great-great-uncle: One thing's for sure, that the intellectuals always made the 'worst soldiers'. Can also unhappily call upon the most celebrated models: even two of our revered German classical authors — Klopstock and Herder — are known to have refused their military service.

[73] Abbreviation for 'Soviet Rocket Service'.

still have much to show you. — You'll get a vertical take-off jet; and you'll be back in the evening on your native banks of the Kalamazoo." —

(But now was the time for caution!: If the scoundrel was supposed to convey this to me on General Coffin's orders — and there seemed no reason to doubt the truth of his hints — then there was nothing else. Rearrange. / Yet at the same time retain my independence and dignity[74]: how to combine the two? . . . / . . . / Here we are. Something like this, eh? (And he, the great car-navigator, had not observed my battle): "Well, Mister Inglefield." (and, apparently concerned, figure it out some more): "No one should be able — on any account! — either on the east — and above all not on the neutral side — to accuse me of lack of objectivity: which would, however, be the case were I not actually to divide my scant time into — at least a very close approximation — of three equal parts! So 17 hours just *have to* be devoted to the port side: or let's say 16; after all, I *am* an American, and no one can hold it against me if I prefer to be where I can make myself" (and a very slight pause did slip out, before I managed to extract the "easily"!) "uh=understood. / So if you could pick me up again from the port-side tomorrow morning round about 9 . . .?"

He pondered businesslike; but otherwise seemed to concur with my thought processes: that was ok to relay to Coffin, yes. / "But then I'd have to be on the other side by 15, at the latest 16 hundred hours this afternoon: so will spend the afternoon there, and the night." (Although on the right side here, they'd sure as hell have laid on a Beauty Queen for me — Oh well, that type, lipstick-'n-lacquered cunts, runs round a dime a dozen back home. Whereas I didn't know Russian ladies from Eve.).

---

[74] Sic! Every reader would have wished the author to have thought of that a hundred pages earlier.

He digested this recital, gnawing his gum the while. Also began, after a few expectant moments, to nod approvingly: "Right. Well: we do have to be objective." / And, right after that: "Good. — So will aim at collecting you tomorrow morning from their 'Krassnaya Gastinitsa'. Or you might come across that short distance on foot: good."

Here lived his house (Inglefield used the grass in front of it so shamelessly as a shoe-brush that I could have boxed his ears on the spot — which I had a considerable desire to do anyway: take it as read!). / (But as usual was in the know as to most important details, the old scoundrel: Bob Singleton, this cruel brute — comparable at most to Edgar Poe — was renowned for the fact that he could sometimes eat 1 whole pound of nougat a day — at one sitting! *Most* odd!).

(I unobtrusively touched my heart: what a Moment!!: I was about to stand, forehead to forehead, opposite the man who had been the very greatest idol of my youth! Quite apart from his only-too-familiar literary monomanias. For a second lumps were scaling up my throat: at his, as at Poe's feet, I would at that instant — have laid down my entire savings in the Great=Rapids=Bank — it is a damned big thing when someone like me, straight from the melting-pot, comes face to face with the history of literature incarnate! I was overawed by the mere thought of the medley of titles of his books.)

I, ready for ministrations of adoration: HE?: firesparks erupted from his shagpipe, reminiscent of Mount Heckelsberg! Stocky was he, in high-necked thin-red jumper and proud as Lucifer: "Ah — You are the expected Journalissimus?"

(Collect yourself: Collect yourself!: This will never happen again!!): And I went all-eyes, all-ears. / My glance raced admiringly-wild through his library?: All manner of oddities, such as one only gets with autodidacts. On the desk, ready to hand, the French Revolution of 1789: "Lamartine!?"; and he nodded matter-of-factly: "Only to be used in conjunction

with Kropotkin." — "Carlyle?"; he took the pipe out of his mouth to speak more vigorously: "Now *there's* a babbler for you!" (Well, I mean to say, the beautiful thing about all these members of the Egghead Republic remains, for all that, that the great dead are treated, opposed, refuted, feuded with, attacked and celebrated as if they were still in the land of the living! — Which, of course, in a certain sense, they are. — For god's sake, if only my brain had worked a little faster!).

Then we sat, grinning glued to our chairs. (On the wall, a never-ending strip of Tieck quotations: so he spoke German!). / "I am weary of the solitude engendered by the company of my friends . . . Chicken-hearts in wolves clothing . . . who maintain that Apollo might as well wear a wig and false teeth: Holy sunset, what a Nation! . . ." (I could only memorize the half of it; and probably 50% of that wrongly — I did what I could).

Fragments (some of what he himself said): "Tradition? : Idlers' sentiments; leaves puddles standing, because they might perhaps derive from the Great Flood." / "I might even, if requested, ferret out some heresies in the Lord's Prayer!". And added, entranced, the following anecdote:

"In Switzerland, where the most pious of folk, all being well, enter a church once a year, roundabout Easter time, an eighty-year old father sent his twenty-five year old son down into the valley for the first time. And when he returned home again, he examined him: what had he seen and heard there? Then the son said to his father: that a chap had spoken, at great length, about another: of how he had been betrayed & sold, captured & bound, drawn & beaten, and finally even crucified. "Yes, father," he said, "so badly was he treated, that it filled me with great pity." / "Good God, Good God!" said the old man thereupon: "Has this business *still* not been settled?! It must be 20 years since I was last in church: they were already dealing with that matter then! I'd like to know what our government is doing, that they do not argue the case out once and for all!" / (And guffawed right heartily).

"*So you've no* so-called 'Religious Feeling'? at all": None at all. Not even as a child! (This kind of thing certainly exists: Voltaire; Diderot; Reimarus; Lessing as well; Kantschopenhauernietzsche; David Friedrich Strauss — a not unimpressive pearl-string of names! : Goethe above all! / And even Bob nodded at that, with hypocritical piety: "If the Lord sendeth Syphilis, He also sendeth penicillin!"). / And the muse had unquestionably kissed him, often and intensively. Above all — God Save Us! — not just with divine inspiration on his forehead, but further south to boot. In the copy of his 'Tandem-trips' he presented to me, he wrote in this very connection: 'Fari quae sentias: Speak what You think.'[75]

Warning: "*Think* it over twenty times before you buy any 'Collected Works'! You will automatically become more careful when you realize that you've landed yourself each time with the entire life of a stranger, a super-destiny: more than you can cope with. — A man who owns more than 1 dozen 'Complete Works' is a charlatan! — Or alternatively: he hasn't read them." / Hadn't much to say in favour of his colleagues: "If one of them can't think of anything new to say, his compositions become suffused with 'Classical Austerity'. / It's always better — as far as I'm concerned — to ask 'Why is he gone?' rather than 'What is he doing here?'!" / "The Island??!! : If you stretched a tent over it, you'd have the biggest circus in the world!". (Plus the sarcastic comment: "*I* do not shirk the responsibilities of my time!"; and, when Inglefield indignantly wagged his mitt: "Sure, sure, I know: I've been 'sworn in': Be still, be silent, my heart!'").

[75] Which the author then unhesitatingly did in this submitted report — and the confused and obscene style of his writing is the result of taking note of such a marvellous maxim: thought is one thing, writing another! / And the heretofore so much fêted Bob Singleton is renowned as one of the most evil so-called 'Erotic Writers', whose books a Christian wouldn't touch with a hot poker: the fact that meetings with Popular Front writers have more than likely taken place in his island home has wisely been omitted by the author! As also that his admission itself was only made possible by the votes of the Eastern Bloc — and, indeed, also the Neutral Bloc.

In front of the door: he had accompanied us (had rung the bell earlier: that he wasn't writing, and the cleaning-woman could start). / Wrinkled his brow and threatened upwards: "Well, most honourable sun?!" (It was already beginning to get a bit hazy, just as predicted by the weather forecast. / 'Fog-powder': only to be handed over to adults. Several kinds; countries where fog flourishes best: Lappland, Luneburg Heath, Maine. Fog-mail-order-house. Fog-*breeders* even? : very good!). —

Lunch; in the hotel beyond Harbour Street: 1 light-grey suit ate with us, blood-red fists (and selfsame elongated shoes; unmistakably 'Miss Alabama'; 5 pinky daggers at the end of each hand). / And gave me one ogling after another, right over the mussel-salad. Her foxy=russet pair of lip=worms kept curling gracefully over their white backdrop. ('I'll have three whores a day, to keep love out of my head.' Otway, if I remember correctly.)[76]

The dance band? : was changed every month. / "As a matter of interest, are many artists vegetarians?" — Their mouths contorted instinctively into just as many smiles: "Hardly ever." / And explain sociologically: they had all originally suffered so much hunger that they systematically stuff themselves like the Prodigal Son. (After all, we devour just about everything: the berries off the plants: all off! The hide off the animals : gone! We suck at every tit; stick every tube in our mouths; the raw mussels of the Seven Seas: just so's we can burp and fart another 10 hours!). / "So I'll leave my luggage here then?". He nodded formally.

An etherial young man stepped gently and bently into the nosherie; ordered 40 ounces of raw minced meat;[77] and then stared apathetically at the wall facing him; 2 brutal eyes in his intelligent face. As he could think of nothing further, he began

---

[76] Thomas Otway, 'The Soldier's Fortune'; Act 1, Scene 3.
[77] Exactly 1134.52 grams.

to employ the long lissom knife as a drumstick — the noble blade hummed and vibrated obediently (and when he started to half-sound the Internationale with inserted trills and warbles, I couldn't contain myself: stood up reverently and bowed to the floor in his direction with downcast eyes, as befits the miserably=ordinary guy who's come into contact with the Absolute. He looked at me with disaffection; his mouth shaped something inaudibly rude (one could tell by the expression of his entire jaw-area); and I bowed once more: to be thus bidden by Great Men is wonderful. (And by Great Women must be more wonderful still!)).

For it was Stephen Graham Gregson! : the author of the 'Police-school', of 'Papa Luna' and the incomparable 'Griffin=Works Ltd' (23 murder-attempts were made on him by textile-entrepreneurs after its publication; 485 prosecutions launched: he'd had to live in the woods for 11 months, hidden by a brave friend — until IRAS finally intervened! At a rally in the large auditorium (broadcast on worldwide TV) all of the then 800 geniuses had stood united behind Gregson. At the same time one of the hallowed snow-white island planes had set off for the swamps of Carolina where the unfortunate Gregson was in hiding at the time — gnashing his teeth and writing like crazy — at first he took it to be a new trick on the part of his persecutors and refused to climb on board (always aided by his minute gaggle of fanatical hangers-on; it had been very difficult to win him over without a struggle!). / And the backwash of public indignation was nearing its climax! Only 1 hour earlier he'd been universally branded an Anarchist and Blasphemer, a Pornographer and a Madman — sounds great, 'Pornographer'; like a profession: 'Photographer'! — Ever since the solemn Island Manifesto, the public immediately turned against the instigators of such a scandalous blunder. A boycott of textiles was proposed (and even carried out for days); so that the disconcerted manufacturers had to do their all to calm down the customers with publicity gimmicks. Of course they succeeded, especially with the women, with no trouble (by presenting fashion flimflam); but the men had been harder to appease: literary historians (of excellent memory for names!) refused for many years to buy their new tuxedos from 'Griffin'! / A further result had been that industrial enterprises no longer employed apprentices with higher education; only relatively simple youngsters meticulously and cunningly tested for their tyrannizability and unwary minimal vocabulary. There also appeared — emanating unobtrusively throughout the land from appropriate legal agencies — carefully worded clauses in small print on apprenticeship contracts: to the effect that the person in question was never, either now or later, permitted to disclose any information regarding his apprenticeship: 'to prevent industrial sabotage'. — Which means, in plain speech, that the government once again allowed itself to be sold down the river[78] in order to cover up the white slave-owners — child labour, as in Charles=Dickens=days!

Still bowing, I was pulled down by Inglefield; began to speak; shook his head; (and the well-trained Miss Alabama withdrew to the powder=potty); he seemed quite thoughtful, even gloomy. / "Strange case: never writes a line any more! — When he first came to the island, piece after piece surfaced from his workshop, each more beautiful and malicious than the last. Then — " (he bent down lower over our plates; mumbled more urgently): — "at one stroke all production ceased! And that was after the following had occurred": (he panted grimly, and bit his own mouth (which I wouldn't like to do if you paid me!)): "At a sportsday — 'Portside versus

---

[78] This whole diatribe of the author's is 'yet one more' proof of his inappropriateness. Mr Gregson has — later generations may judge — an indisputably nice talent, which nonetheless lies mouldering in the swamp : the swamp of unbridled lusts. His above-mentioned novel about the American textile industry proves nothing other than that he belongs to that class of people which can't reconcile themselves to an orderly middle-class occupation: apprenticeship and military service never did anyone any harm!

Starboard' — Gregson had fallen for a Russian woman — one of those squat square types who can do pull-up and forward-roll with one hand on the horizontal bar." (I looked across: he held his head close over the unbelievable mountain of meat, and chomped with the greed of a wolf): "Perhaps it was just the contrast?" I guessed: "because he is so thin? Of course: love transfer: he stuffs himself like that because he wants to be like her!". But Inglefield shook his head disbelievingly): "You don't know everything yet; hold your assumptions a while. — At first they met 'Beyond the Gates'. The impudent=sinister creature enticed him further and further. Until he came to her in the Left Library, where of course he met more Russians. Then finally he claimed: that he had to spend 6 or 8 weeks over there for preliminary work on a new novella — there's nothing you can do; officially we are powerless then." Pause, he chewed with exasperation.

"*And=uh: unofficially?*" *I was emboldened* to ask. "Oh, unofficially unofficially!" he snorted irritably: "unofficially of course we tried all sorts of things; subtle advice from acquaintances. Respectful invitations to a lecture — tour through the States — but he always made excuses: they aren't worthy of him! / All WACs were given orders to make a play for him: whoever succeeded in getting him away from that Russian would have her salary doubled and her contract extended — In vain! : And some of those girls are so interesting . . .!" Slammed his mouth shut (and obviously thought of a sculptress by the name of Berta Sutton, what a woman, yeah. And I couldn't really disagree with Gregson there. (Or maybe; for Bertie was 'interesting' in a certain sort of way. Very much so in fact. Although as a woman she lacked just about everything. Except for one thing perhaps.)).

"*So he went over to the other side: 4 weeks;* 6 weeks: 8 weeks! — Then he came back: just as you see him now. — / He no longer writes; he doesn't work. If you ask him he repeats the same hackneyed dictum: all of Western literature is — well, you know what."

He leant towards my ear; he whispered with a gravy-soaked voice: "Of course we have interrogated him under hypnosis: *he just is not the same man!!* His vocabulary has diminished in some incomprehensible way; and his American which he's lost has by no means been replaced by newly acquired Russian; no! He has the mentality of a peasant boy!"

Full of food, he raised himself higher; he crossed his lanky arms over his chest; and pierced me with his glance:

"*And that is why, Mister Winer,* I must now officially entreat you: keep your eyes open over there — as wide as possible: *something has happened, you see!* / And this is not the only case of its kind: Miss Jane Cappelman" (he saw from my respectfully open features that I knew of the lyric poet and saved himself the explanation): "she too runs around in Poet's Corner — similarly 'entranced'. She too has fallen for an irresistible bald-headed Tularussian; she too had to study the life and work in the People's Republics — she too has gone silent: we've measured her vocabulary; at the last count it was 380!". / Departure. (Sniffy=nosed, Miss Alabama gave me her polished right: because I hadn't unconditionally capitulated before her charms). —

Outside: sky dense with dark cloud-ruins: Flyability of the leaves on the increase. / We stood next to one another and waited for the Russian car scheduled to collect me. / The manager's huge Siberian wolfhound joined us playfully, tail-wagging. So Inglefield instantly grabbed a pebble and threw: *but at the animal!* — "Hey?! What's the big idea?" I cried outraged (now I could repay the old boy a home-run or two: 'Prevention of Cruelty to Animals'); and coaxing: "Nowcome — Jeees; come to me! — There . . ." (and he did come trustingly up to my side; I threw a little stick for him: joyfully barking he tore after it, (with a force sufficient to chase a wayward bull!). Then he brought the stick back, very proud, and laid it at my feet. Sat down beside me, the hairs on his back standing up stiff as thorns (so tall was he that I had to bend my arm at a right angle to put my hand on his head!). I scratched him; and precociously he looked down the road with me. / Inglefield had apologized nervously: he couldn't stand that breed any longer. Even gave a sort of explanation: a similar wolfhound — "perhaps bigger *still*" — had strayed into Bertie Sutton's hands; and, being a typical sculptress she had been delighted by the splendid model (and made nothing but dogs for 4 weeks; one of the results being the famous 'Reading' — a haggard virgin has received her 1st love letter, and reads it with touching joy to her former giant playmate: he gives ear so attentative=sulkily as if he could jealously understand every word! — had been a real hit with philistines; and Springfield, the town, had immediately purchased it and put it in the public park: the maidens there were her spittin' image!). / Anyway, she'd dragged the beast around everywhere with her. "Even at my place, and=uh-a —" I just nodded; he continued more nervously: "The next morning I couldn't find a couple of — not all-that-important, but still=uh — confidential orders from the Administration of our side. Never found them again either." / "Bertie didn't have them, of course; although I had to agree to her 'screening' —" (under hypnosis); his eyes shimmered transfigured: "Mind you, it was pretty shocking because=uh: You know . . ." (and I nodded again: I know): "but she just kept on confessing purely and simply: Oh Senecy: I love you sooo! — Lovely isn't it?". (So he is called 'Seneca': that was all I needed!). He continued more soberly: "Well. The next morning 4 acquaintances who had been to the theatre the evening before, gave evidence: they had seen a huge hound-like shape in the bright moonlight when they were driving past the gallery and library into Poulaphouca Street, dashing past them with something white in its mouth; and, crossing the Neutral Strip, had streaked along 'Literature Street' into the Eastern sector! ? They had, admittedly, all been 'high' — " he added, sighing . .

He looked into the distance, his tubular limbs lolling loose in their fittings; he started to say: "Hardly anyone ever dies over there any more. Only by accident. The number of 'red' deaths in the last 10 years amounted to a total of 4!" (He shooed away all the things I wanted to babble about, like a stupid fly; he had more important things to say): "The fact is you are *not* going over purely as a private citizen . . ." (just then a capacious black limousine turned in, down where Right Street and Harbour Street intersect. A deep growling tone came from the dog's chest. Inglefield spoke more softly, also more quickly): "If anyone *should* make you any sort of offer — even if it's only an intimation — : '*Yes indeed! ; We have something to swap!!*'. — Have I made myself clear?!!"

"*Uh=yes — sure —* " *I stuttered* numbly. Then pulled myself together; I shouted: "Mister Inglefield: Who are you?!" — He answered casually: "The Chief of United Western Island Intelligence." / But then the alien car was already stopping in front of us.

They icily touched the rims of their hats, as if they were drawing daggers, saluting each other, Mister Inglefield and Comrade Uspenski (who right away gave the dog a kick so that it scampered howling away — which endeared the animal to me even more). / Then I sat in the backseat betwixt 2 figures, the like of whom I'd only seen before in propaganda films (and back along Harbour Street at a furious tempo, smack around the Town-Hall: over the boundary of 'Left Street' — and then they slowed down; breathed more deeply; and tilted their hats up at ease). / "Yes, please: nice and slowly." (I was still pretty numbed: so that bastard, that Inglefield, had been tailing me all along. Would do so again tomorrow. (And I really became frightened: on what kind of dragon's scaly tail had I trodden this time! Had thought it was a harmless playful lizard about whom one could report a few delightful sweet nothings. — : What was I supposed to say, if the occasion arose? : that Inglefield would have something to *swap*?!).). —

"What is that over there?": I had not, in the course of my thinking, overlooked the mighty monument which towered aloft hard by 'Literature Street': "May I take a peep at it?". And he smiled, broad and broad-shouldered: "Bot off-corrse!"

'Monuments of the Russians'?: I strode around the 3 metre high pedestal: Warriors, Banners, Armoured Riders; Riders in Armoured Cars? — : "It glorifies the military victories of our Great Soviet Union."

"Could you perhaps translate a couple for me?" (For the inscriptions were in Cyrillic, and my little Greek didn't help out at all. I pointed at one at random; and he read out):

"Josef Vissarionovitch Djugashvili rose onto a ranting red steed; swelled under the sheen of a bushy helmet; splendiferously splurged a weighty spearhead — : after 1200 days Germany was to be the GDR." / (So had again stumbled on a 'German Corner', seems to be my Kismet; here, now this one): "From Konrad to Adenauer the Germans went on 10 campaigns against Russia: 4 against hovels; 2 for show; 2 to rescue; 2 to conquer; not one victorious; the last one with no return." / (Very pithy, wouldn't you agree? This third one, please): "Stalingrad: They came; saw; and fled." (And elephantine clouds — spreading their tentacles — shoved each other over the skies: had there still been Germans, they would have looked real ninnies[79]. / Stand next to the car and have a look-see. (My wrist at my ear, lusting: "Sixteen hundred hours." : So thankgod, absolutely punctual!). / But: "Who on earth is *that* lot there?":

[79] Yet another example of the author's almost obsessive dislike of the former Germany. Unfortunately in this particular case he can refer to the fact that it was about the special 'Hitlergermany' — an alibi behind which our fatherlandless fellows used to love hiding in the old days.

All in step: that's the way the groups came marching up! Nine at a time (oh yes, that's right: ten or more is forbidden on the island — and not only for technical reasons either!); all in battle-tunics; defiantly without headgear; some wore jack-boots? . . .

But he warded off the answer again: that flankman there — — — : "Isn't that — : Busslayev?". And Comrade Uspenski nodded proudly: "Da" (So they *do* have a word for 'yes' after all!). / And the further explanation: "Those are our writers. Who march united into the library every morning, and again after the midday siesta." / (Yes, indeed: the first troupe had just arrived: File left! — and straight away they vanished stiffly through the folding door.) / (And our Western mammoth libraries stand empty: all funny here; as ours is sad!).

This 'Trade Union Literature': 3 giant blocks; a hundred metre frontage, thirty high: "ziss way iff you please?" —

First the printing works downstairs? And he nodded offhand: "For domestic use: internal stuff." / Apart from this, of course, the gigantic printing house in the Neutral Strip serviced this part as well; 500,000 copies of each book were produced, to be snapped up immediately by the eagerly waiting outside world: one of the *very* big sources of income on the island. No wonder it 'held its own financially' — probably did even better than that!).

"Secretaries' offices over there — hang on: I'll just get the interpreter assigned to you for the duration of your stay — whom you can also use any time for your private work: and — the like". / And was back at once; next to him the Kamchatka-lily in question: short build, with the arms of a wrestler, and five inches more round the shoulders than me: "Comrade Yelena Kovalevna: Mr Winer, who is going to do a report on us — " and smiled over the entire breadth of his face: "So let's make an eefoort, shall we Comrade!". / She moved next to me in silence (and that was when I really got an eyefull: wow, did

that woman have a bosom! Could it be real?! — Comrade Uspenski had followed my gaze, and nodded proudly: "Grrreat.")

And very decent office equipment! There was nothing missing. (The adding machine was even bigger than our current models; I calculated wagging my chin; and then Comrade Yelena (or does one say Kovalevna?) spoke for the first time: "Fifteen places."[80] she confirmed. / Uspenski disappeared momentarily.

Down echoing labyrinths, corridors and railed staircases. She ambled noncommittally beside me; hands — whose grip of a mere handshake had given me a lot to think about, behind her back. (Perhaps it would be better if I spent the night on the other side after all, with our people? No; no deal; nutten doin': I'd have to be the worthy representative of the Free West, in all its strength, with the Fair Helena as well. Victim of my chosen objectivity.)

Sound of scrambled murmurs here? : She nodded. "Cadre 8 is fulfilling its novel-quota." And a little more softly: "They have fallen behind. Neblagonadezhni." / I forebore to ask what that cool noise was supposed to mean;[81] but I did inquire: "D'you think we could have a peep?"

"I'll ask." — *She vanished.* (instantly it went quiet in there for a bit. — But then a voice started up again, interruptions followed and Yelena waved me in from the opened door):

In the Conference Room (because that's what it looked like, more or less: a long horseshoe-shaped table. At the head of it, next to a speed-writing=maiden, a tough-looking gentleman with a goatee. 4 writers on either side, listening intently; so 8 altogether, 3 of them women). / We remained standing discreetly in the doorway; I bent down to lend Yelena my ear,

---

[80] 'Fifteen decimal places'.
[81] Unreliable.

and she whispered the translation powerfully via her mighty mammaries. (It's virtually impossible to deceive deliberately in a case like this: hardly anyone can lie that quickly on the spur of the moment; particularly into a foreign language.) / In between hasty answers to questions: the novel was set in a department store: which, at this point, towards the end, and symbolically enough, had caught fire! — The goatee up front clenched his fist — (he was in fact in charge of the structure) — and read aloud:

'*He staggered in through the door* and observed . . .': "Stop! Nyet! No! Rubbish! Madness!" simultaneous cries poured at once from every quarter. The young lady with the black fringe jumped up and shouted: "Impossible! : If he's 'staggering' it's rabid nonsense to talk about an 'observation'! What he would do is 'scream': or 'gasp', 'yell', um=. . ." (her fingers picked at pockets in the air for further possibilities.) / "Gurgle?" suggested someone; and the man next to him thoughtfully ventured, "gur=gelled — ". / "But *what* has he got to observe?" asked a rational man; but the Fringe jumped up again: "Don't! I can't bear to hear that word any more!" "But whyyyh?" the quiet one countered, amazed. — And she obviously told him: that they were not unobserved. And even if it was only by a Dumb Dog 'who didn't speak the lingo!' (Of course I only guessed the latter from her mini=gesticulations and 1 furious look: !). "Let's go: I don't want to cause a disturbance on any account." / (Into the Corydon again; inside the weary battle of words wore on wildly. And at that point the literature cadres were experimenting on the theme of macro=organisms: "There are two prototypes of organisms which are the lot of mankind: the one-family house — and the 'macro-organization': this is the place for communal production — the former, after fulfilled quotas, for individualism." They were describing to the best of their ability the 'macro-organization' of a bank; a head post-office; department store, barracks, school; factories of all kinds, broadcasting station, local government office, funfairs. One man had even added 'parliament' to the programme, but that was struck off again by the trade union leadership.)

"*So you really believe* that a work of art could be produced collectively?" — : "*Dada,* but of course!" she replied, surprised. / And was so thoroughly refuted, I could barely hold my own: Beaumont & Fletcher. The 'Xenien' by Goethe & Schiller! Claude Lorrain?: others had painted in the figures. / "Plagiarism: what is it, in the last analysis, if not self-knowledge? That the person concerned lacks what he takes from others? There just *do* happen to be — shall vee zay — great psychologists, who have no feeling whatsoever for the beauties of nature: must the treatment of landscape in their books therefore remain inadequate?: How foolish!"./ "And the author's name on the completed novel?": "Cadre 8" she confirmed cheerfully. / "But doesn't a work of art put together like this ultimately miss out on — : unity? Consistency of thought-processes?": "You mean 'the limitation of the individual'?" she instantaneously reformulated : "The limitation of his talent? — An individual person is never complete: we try to fill his gaps. Through careful selection and permutation of related, but differently talented, minds: additive!" / (And gave further most interesting details about assembling such artist-combines: it was certainly not haphazardly undertaken! They all had to have the same — shall we say phlegmatic — temperament; the same blood group; similar childhood impressions and environmental experiences. But they would differ in their special endowments: one would excel at powerful action; the other at aphorisms of the most sublime profundity. The third a phenomenal memory machine for colourful vocabulary. The young lady with the fringe was — she confided, blushing playfully — the 'Erroteek Specialist'.)

That was my springboard for daring innuendo!: "By the way, what is the Russian for 'I love you'?" I asked by-the-by. She wrinkled her muscular brow; but must have remembered her duty and replied with ominous flirtatiousness: "Ya tebyá lublyúh." (And I yatebyalublyuhted until I knew it backwards).

"*May I know* what this here means?": the little frame on the corridor wall looked splendidly tasteful, with its lightly tinted paper and the ornate lettering. Slowly but effortlessly she translated the angular curlicue:

> 'When a Russian poet kills,
> he atones for it, if the victim was a Yank
> with 10 roubels — a Latin American
> with 20 — an Arab, Indian, Chinaman
> with 500 roubels — or 3 typewriters
> with ribbon, two erasers
> and a thousand sheets of flimsy, type DIN A 4.'

My face must have shown horror, because she laughed briefly, sprightly and purred with good humour: "Just a leettle joke — : *You* are our guest; our honoured guest." (Nonetheless: charming maxims! But she:) "It's from an old novel — middle of the century — by Comrade Ivan Mikhailovitch Afanasyev." (Her fangs articulated the grandiloquent nomenclature just like that — no sweat!)

Uppermost storey; at once a notice ordered Silence!: "Chess!" (The qualifying tournament for World Championship candidates. We crept in soundlessly. This time she just *wrote* the names on her pad out of respect, and then pointed with the tip of her pencil at the person in question:!). / And there they all sat: Galachov and Kareyev; Fortunatov and Velyaninov = Sernov; Spasovitch and Slavatinski; a sparkling string made up of the most illustrious names. (Although I'd imagined Comrade Fortunatov to look muchmuch older: he was pushing a hundred; and yet came second in every match! Definitely still a tough old breed, these Russkies: stocky, with silver-grey beard; I'd have guessed him to be 60 *at the most*.) /

And now the score: the first 34 places were held by the Soviet Russians. Then 2 former Yugoslavs (who must have been pretty ancient too; I couldn't recognize their faces because they were hunched so intently over the board.) Then followed 1 Czech and 4 Argentinians. / The only Yankski lay way back in 42nd place (and in the process of losing again; he was three pawns down. I shook his compatriotic hand in sympathetic silence.) / (He got up and pulled me over to the window: "We are being gypped!" he hissed: "I am playing against a sort of 12-year old: who's supposed to be Stassyulevitch. But I know him from way back: and it ain't him! Granted, he plays just like him: the same favourite opening, the same goddam tricks. And recognized me at once; drivelling on about a 're-juvenation treatment'!"). / Yelena with casual pride: "We've just filed an application for the admission of 4 more Grand-Masters to the island: grreat." / But then, with an ultra-deadly flicker: "Although our two stars went missing! . . . " And I glanced disconcertedly at the man on the first board:?: True enough! He wasn't the world-runner-up Voveyko. And the World Champion was likewise nowhere to be seen: "But he doesn't need to join the game." ? She wanted to scream at me. She remembered where we were; she hissed: "Do you have to be told twice?!: The great Ryleyev and Voveyko are ...". She got herself under control; she finished off contemptuously: "... not prrresent." / Over, out & downstairs. —

In the open air: the clouds had by now gotten quite dense. / And I presented my little plan: "I should have liked to get to know the ancient A.F. Stupin personally — at least to have set eyes on him just once." — (I had always enjoyed reading his 'Quiet Donna'.) / And truly amazing luck: just across the way the cadres were marching back from the library! — "He's in that column: I'll give him a shout."

And a tall frisky girl with a gay = blonde sash of hair, jumped out from the very back row. Towards us. Guttural words rolled back and forth — then she slugged my shoulder like a tomboy and offered me her hand:! (I was disappointed; but bowed nevertheless, and replied politely: "Pleased to meet you, Mrs. Stupin." (Had the interpreter misunderstood me after all! — Ahwell, fuckit: I can still write 'the bubbly glowing wife of the ancient Titan'[82]; or some such porridge. — They were still laughing; once again the merry corn-sprite eyed me enterprisingly; once again the farewell-slap on my left arm — then she nimbly closed ranks with her cadre.)). / "So Mrs Stupin writes as well?"; but Yelena just chuckled with amusement; and kept on shaking her short thick hair (until I caught it too; giggled with her; lifted my forefinger and repeated emphatically: "Ya / tebyá / : lublyúh!". And she, throatily: "Goodd.").

Over there the Redchinese? — *I hesitated:* after all, we still hadn't quite recognized China yet. — (On the other hand I am supposed to feign objectivity!). / But she made it easy for me, with surprising sensitivity: "Let's go to the Dancers' Union" she proposed: "there are many people there."

And right through the middle of the 'Kremlin', the colossal department store with a dome: crystal Vodka-bottles. Black dunes of caviar. — Sheer delight: ladies' floating-chemisette! : teeny weeny night-panties; plus a light bell-shaped mini-smock to waft over it. ('Saving on material' whispered a sceptical Western spirit in my ear; and there was only the one pattern. She observed that the gear had done the trick for me.) / "May I buy a couple of things?": "But please, do choose! —: Whatever your heart desires. You are our guest!"

So I took a loud checked notepad here. A brown=red typewriter ribbon there. / Hey: that was interesting! (And worth recommending! She explained the reference books to me. — All of them single-volume: a simple Dictionary of Orthography. The People's Encyclopaedia. The Higher Encyclopaedia

---

[82] 'The tall, verÿ youthful young wife of the Siberian Titan' is the final version for the series for publication.

(with supplements for the intellectuals: its entry for 'Napoleon' sure looked pretty different from the one in the 'People's'! That abounded in popular phrases, about the 'yoke of the Corsican'; this one had names, dates, numbers in rapid succession: I'd never found such cleverly worked-out biogrammes at home!). (But the 'ordinary man in the street' wouldn't have been able to do anything with it: ah, that is the distinction, after all!: Which we're unfortunately still loth to make; or rather, to accept. — She sensed my reluctant appreciation and proudly craned her bull's neck: Little Mother Russia!)).

(But must choose with moderation!: otherwise these people will think that we don't even have pencils — though no doubt that's drummed into them anyway!). A snack in the eating-area. — The hot sausage was — ?: yes = indeed; not bad at all. / The fish fillet? — : crisp and large. / China tea & golden plums from Turkistan?: a real treat for the Dumb Dog?!—

Dancers' Union: at first the hall was shrouded in black; excepting a lot of scene-changing on stage. We sat down, side by side, in the front row (so close that I exercised my only Russian phrase; and she nodded matter-of-factly: it'll come in time.) / House walls stood pell-mell (one upside-down: that did look pretty bad). A glaring artifical tree sprawled diagonally across its foundling-stone on which Prince Igor could easily have rested when the curtain rises. / Stage-managers swore (one of them out of sight); workers hung at the slip-knot cables; a poodle sat intensely on its hind legs; the lighting engineer spared no effort.

With eyes closed: that's how the Chinese damsel wafted onto the stage! Arms sprouted yellow from her body; legs closely rotated around her. She made herself small, and emitted a virginal-mindless titter (in relation to which her long back looked out of place; she was obviously aware of that, and seldom showed it): Nope! / To the left?: 'Pa = da = linn:

Pa=da=linn' pluck-noted the balalaika; and weightlifter women, dressed up as daughters of the Komsomols, tripped out for the dance of the roundelay: in my dubious honour. (All of them were blessed with the identical physique; the same as my girl=guide's in fact: "Wonderful"; I moaned, as sensuously as I could; and she nodded, reassured.)

A patter behind us: Comrade Uspenski reappeared; Watched with us for a moment; and just smiled at the thought of American women: "They may be experienced; but they aren't solidly=stacked like the wenches from our steppes." (Too right: Yelena had some backside — I'd be well bushed after a bit of that... Well, no matter: Vogue la Galère!). —

Whatever am I supposed to do in that Machine Area of theirs? — But he seemed so eager to show it off (and I also recalled Inglefield's hints of the morning), that I did him the favour. —

Through the little park: the trees grew noticeably higher than those over on our side! (Did they have better methods of irradiation here? Or with transplants already? I angrily kicked with my toe-cap at an impudently=well-shaped pebble.) / Or again, the playing field: "Considerably larger than that of the Starboard terrain." And he replied with provocative certainty: "Dó=bble.". / And further, the harbour had vermillion=illuminated sky-signs to match the ruddy lighthouse. In contrast to the capitalists' whitey-green. (As in fact they differentiated constantly, between nalyevo and napravo.)[83]

Again the same machine quarter; and more of the same mammoth rotation. Piston-rods assaulted me: very close shave! I was being cog-wheeled blackandyellow; condensing coils hissed; one light cone after another was being trained on and over me. (And those muscles all the time!) / The hundred-word-goons: for that was how Uspenski quite openly described the Herculean apes to me: was I then a sort of go-between? A

---

[83] Russian for 'right' and 'left'.

mediator, unintentionally, a contact man? Runner, agent, intermediary, middleman, Ragnarök? (One of them had a constellation of oil-trickles in his stand=up hair, which was lit up from behind; but had never seen the light of day, for all that. Pit-horses. (but those, at any rate, must have been blind, which this one here was not allowed to be.).).

"*Yelena: Sslushai!*":[84] They jabbered for a little while: suppose they ever hit on the idea of conquering the whole island?! (But then I recalled Inglefield, that cool customer. What had he said?: He had something to swap? — There was a great power behind me! (And in front of me too!: I started to shudder. And it was with definite relief that I heard them enunciate a familiar word — 'Stupin'; and promptly tuned in): —):

"*We'll show it to him* — : *Uh=please come.* — "

Back. Along 'October Revolution Street'. That over there was the MTS, i.e., the 'Machine=Tractor=Station', from which the 'Fields & Pastures' on the left were cultivated. / "Oh, we haff too!" : i.e., a green belt, 'Beyond the Gates', the 'Collective Solitude' (where their great men relaxed in the country air; drinking Crimean wine and milk from Kasakstan. Took Spartan Eurotas=baths; rested as prescribed and became young again.)

"*Yongk ah=gain*" *he repeated,* glad of the cue (and *such* inviting hand-jugglery): "Our Clinic.": / (And gently hazy evening: dusk swathing the building now; twilight invites me, mist entices me.)

On the wall, right next to the entrance, the life-sized relief of a giant Siberian wolfhound (3 columns for names beneath it; 2 of them already filled in — may be meant to be in the style of those former St Gotthard=St Bernard dogs? They who had saved human lives in the icy Tundras?). —

[84] 'Listen a minute!'

In a laboratory: Uspenski was trying to persuade the little white-armoured hero, who was supposed to be guiding us (and was apparently raising objections; time and again, with such tenacity that eventually Uspenski snatched some writing materials from out of his breast-pocket and curtly gave him what for. The laboratory assistant standing by signed as witness (at which I noticed that he had a pencil-thin brown dough-sticklet in his hand: wasn't that . . . : Of course, god!: it was the 'Welcome' from yesterday! So they were examining it here — suspiciously and chemically.) / (But funny as it was, I was distressed: so this was the life on the 'Sacred Island of Humanity'?! I just can't stomach that word 'sacred' — which I had always mistrusted anyhow — ever again!)).

"Professor Shukovski.": *we bowed to one another,* as by custom ordained. Once again he questioned with a mute side-glance: once again Uspenski let his hands do the confirmatory forward roll. Whereupon the former finally shrugged his firm shoulders and went ahead.

In the hospital ward: only 2 beds, in which a couple of very pale people were lying. The Professor explained; Yelena translated (faltering; because many technical terms cropped up).

So it was true after all, what had been rumoured abroad in the rest of the world: the Russians were going in for organ transplants! Here 2 ageing administrators were having their worn-out hearts replaced by fresh ones! / "Taken out of whom?" / (I forced myself to use male objectivity. And allegedly they had been sturdy youths, fatally injured in car accidents, "and such like." (Yes quite: "and such like"! But didn't pursue the interrogation.)). / "And by how much do you prolong the life-span of the people concerned?". 30 years. — "And the operation succeeds?": in 90% of all cases.

Outside, Uspenski elaborated smugly: that of course they went in for systematic breeding selection as well: poet on poetess; sculptor on sculptress: "In 300 years time they will look down on us in the way we look down on gorillas now." / My misgiving: "Does poet plus poetess really add up to poet to the power of 2?" But Professor Shukovski intervened: "The speech centre is measurably enlarged every time." (That had me beaten again. — "But supposing he lacks the suitably favourable environment, that infant prodigy?" — They just smiled: "We take care of that.").

Then an overall was slipped on me, white as the snow of Verchoyansk; a stiff disinfected baker's cap up top; carbolic mask over my mouth. Even Uspenski showed only a smiling brow; one of Yelena's eyes gazed deep, the other flat. (Amid monsters the only feeling breast.)

In the operating theatre: I was an old hand at that, hardened from earlier reporting assignments. / But things were briskly different here!: on the double-occupancy operating table the two semi-corpses — beside each, on top, the hairy skull-case. 2 white devils were snipping away like mad in the cavities; incomprehensible monosyllabic noises came from their muslin-snouts...: and then each held a fat grey brain in the red rubber-gloves: they changed places...: and stuffed them inside again! / (And knotted and shouted for fresh artery couplings, for more blood and cat — Uspenski took my one elbow, the Professor the other; Yelena shoved from behind) —

— —

and then we were standing outside again: I ripped off the sterilized rag; I screamed: "Does it work?!". (This brain-transplant. I knew perfectly well what our doctors can get up to with Leucotomies; but the entire brain....?): "That's just impossible!" : "For Sovietpeeple there is no 'eempossible'." he corrected me sternly. / And it worked: if an important Russian writer or scientist began to age, his priceless brain was (at around 60) inserted in a young athlete of 20: "Can you imagine? : he thrives! Writes poeseee — Oh, of luv!". (And carried on working for another 40, 50 years; expanded his

experience; with his vocabulary forever on the increase......
— : "But he must look quite different?!" (Although of course that wasn't a serious objection to the method as such; he then weakened it further: "We take guys who are as similar as possible." (Must take that down at once: Short story: 'He resembled him too closely'!) — Then Satan inspired me: "Of course the sons would be the most similar?"[85] And he did grant me a positive nod, thoughtfully=thinlipped. Fathers & Sons!).

And I promptly had to lean against the wall: they closed in on me, in an expectant semi-circle; and Yelena interpreted, with her mouth still muted by tulle: "Wassa matter, dear?" / I swallowed several times. I brought it out: "Yelena! — : in that case... that just now... *was* Stupin after all?!". / She laughed and proceeded to tell to the other two the anecdote about how I'd said 'Mrs Stupin'. Uspenski grinned "Goodd"; and Shukovski, the expert: "No trouble: one can also transplant the brain of a man into the body of a girl. Comrade Stupin needed many 'feminine feelings' for his new novel=hexalogy, and after much careful thought decided upon a woman's body." / (So *that's* how he achieved the masterly evocation of maidenly thought-processes! Hence those unbelievable powers of empathy, the understanding of awkward=graceful girly=capriciousness: hence finally the exciting description of the great defloration in Volume 4, which even our envy-grinders had to salute as inimitable: no wonder if the guy had himself been both, youth *and* maiden!).

(*Tiresias: still up against the wall:* the Problem of Tiresias! He was supposed to have been both as well (and had given evidence: it was even *more* fun as a woman!). / Or Thorne Smith, with his 'Turnabout'!).

---

[85] This tone of the modern desperado is typical of the author and his profession: trains of thought which earlier generations would never have conceived of are not just considered, but are fecklessly caught on to and expressed — irrespective of the outcome.

"Come: let's eeeat": they had nerves of steel! / — "Can I get a dose of fresh air first please?". — They calmly opened their hands: but of course. (The Professor took his leave: till tomorrow morning.)

Between the clinic and the MTS: Oh No!: what a terrible thought! (And the wide pastures lay so peaceful in the misty vapour. Ripe fields resounded with the rattle of the bird scarer: no rest for the wicked.) But it was this:

"So what do you do — if I may ask — with the organs of the 'young people'? Whose bodies you have transbrained?". And, sighing heavily, answered myself: "Just throw 'em away." "Oh no, pleeze," Uspenski reassured me good-humouredly: "They aren't wasted: tomorrow morning; before you leave. We still have *lots* to show you." (And again the black eye-cherries were laughing: there's a surfeit of the Oriental in these guys; you just can't fathom them.) / Still, beautiful, that wide view over the weald: the boundary of the forest was nearly 1 mile away. Must have needed it, as steppe-replacement; on our side there were trees dotted around everywhere, park-like, 'I feel, as after rainfall, a park would, by my house'. (Well, no: *I* didn't feel like that at this particular moment!).

Back along 'October Revolution Street': "In that case one could also — in theory! — put together a superbrain?: The unerring eye of a painter; the speech-centre of a poet; a composer's ear?". (Or, more generally: combine the shoulders of a boxer with the stomach of an ostrich, the etcetera of a tigress?). He lifted his high shoulders higher still: "It *is* a problem. — But you will have to ask Comrade Shukovski about that tomorrow: I don't know."

At the reserved corner-table of the 'Krassnaya Gastinitsa': "The comrade was a Stachanovka in shorthand and American." (Yelena in fact; we three sat down together.) (And better change the subject; one could clean it up by giving it dinner-talk colouring, but it didn't really go with divinely = raw roast beef and the brain-sized dollop of mashed potatoes.)

Table-talk: About the 'Russki Film', the good 'un. / About the lazy West: "Many of your artists apply of their own accord to be sent home again: they say there's not enough 'going on'!" (And I had to admit it, against my will; it had happened.) / How they, the Russians, had pushed through the notion that either the Western law about blasphemy should be complemented by another about 'Blasphemy against Atheism' or both offences should be abolished as trifling: "They *were* abolished". (Since then the Island churches and = temples were allowed only if they looked like ordinary houses; the Christian ones, for instance, with a very inconspicuous little cross 'not offensive to the eye' in the gable. — "Yes; I did get to hear about the bell-ringing business." And they gurgled cheerfully: "Yorr Healthsk".) / But I only partook of the good vodka with immense caution; I had a few further plans for today. / (Although I really had lost my appetite! I turned towards La Belle Hélène; I asked with some urgency: "Are you still...?" — She understood me immediately, nodded earnestly, and replied: "I am still I." (Mind you: 'still'!). / "Your health, Mister Uspenski!" (He smiled and tolerated the foreign title. Was now beaming roundly. 'And his Mrs Dolly boozed like a porter' — namely Yelena: "Yorr Healthsk!" / Then renewed accusations against the Wild West: hadn't the old NATO in its day attempted to hold meetings on the island?! Because, so they said, 'the amenities were so ideally suitable' there?: it was refused by the Eastern Bloc and the Neutral votes. (And it was, if that was true — and I didn't doubt it: the old NATO had enough cheek for that! — just another pathetic example of how the West could never compromise itself enough. The East & Centre were clever enough always to let us make our blunders first, until the Neutrals threw up as soon as they as much as heard our name — and then the Reds moved in — Inglefield could say what he liked: we were powerful but dumb! — Intelligent, even, if you like; sporting; brilliant technologists; the most talented sculptors, like Bertie Sutton: but so dumb with it!: "Yorr healthsk, Grashdanihn Winarr!" — (Now he was paying me back for my 'Mister' earlier on!)).

But watch out; for Ghengis Khan-type barbarity kept showing through. In the acrid vinegar. In the spiced Baikalic seals'-liver. : "Sugarr? : be good!" was her admonishment when the cube didn't want to drop straight into her cup. (In half-Russian: so their word comes from 'sacharine'. And I got up: someone pass this man a bed!). —

Suite of rooms with bed: her wide-splayed lids. / First she pointed it all out to me with providential care: "Vánnaya: Ubórnaya."[86] (emphatically. And I — making an effort: "Ya. Tebja. Lublyuh.").

Sharpandsweetsnogging: her breasts were real! The flutterchemisette of the Ssecretarsha or Perevottshitsa pulled over her head (*and* furthermore an 'honoured champion sportswoman' yet: O what poor mortals we!). / Her mouth tasted of smoky vodka. She pinched me with yellow fingers, and I heard her growl. (Something about 'karottki' and 'tonnki'; through a hole in her Mongol-dial).

In the snowy reaches of her breasts (Tale of the Ragged Mountains). / Her Tundra of a stomach (I was 'lenihvy' she growled: 'sskarreye!'.[87] (And those brains kept interposing their shadows in my head: it wasn't pure joy all the way!)).

Boilinghot rum with butter: that's what she served up with the tonic (plus an aphrodisiac-pickled footbath: how about that: da capo!):

---

[86] Bath and W.C.
[87] It cuts against the grain of my moral feelings of responsibility to translate the relevant Russian expressions; thanks be to God it is not necessary in this instance — for the 'local colour' of which the author is so enamoured is actually all the better sustained this way.

In the pumpkin-gardens of her breasts ('Night-chalet in the pumpkin gardens': now where did I remember that from?).[88] Her honey-toned maiden's arse (probably unwashed; I: a crawler swimming on sprawling-gasping transplantable flesh: of course *that* idea put the kibosh on it!) / She left me, shaking her head.

Black rain falls by night. Trees swaying negroid (with negro-leaves?): at night I'm a dark man!

And this night?! — : *There's* an etching by my special friend Hogarth, in which the ill-doer is having his entrails taken out in a technoid hell made up of operating theatres (a horned-nimble mini-devil squatting on the floor packs them into a barrel): his ribs stick out; his brain's drilled into: why did you torment your fellow men so much?! / And that's just how I felt: creatures invaded me, such as I hope never to set eyes on again: tufty-boobed trollops, thorns encircling the appropriate holes; two-headed man-dogs. Seals singing anthems (and *their* facial desolation ought to have been photo=captured!). / Until one of my recurring dreams almost released me: woods in which LilliandI were straying. (And a robbers' den with knives; which we escaped, as usual.) The landscape became more beautiful; leafier and lonely. We raised our feet and floated across a lake-basin: gone. The woodlands hotter, sunnier, more youthful, more dam-like, blue boats and yellow water (which again perfectly matched Cooper's 'Glimmer-Glass': I've always considered him a great man). Blue & Yellow. / (But then again the 'Wall of the Universe' — which I'll have to describe later on sometime; it's not to everybody's taste. Though not entirely disagreeable.) —

---

[88] Isaiah: 1,8. / The — quite unnecessarily! — quoted Luther translation is, moreover, an error at this stage; the correct version is 'observation platform in a cucumber field': which renders the author's lecherous association of ideas utterly redundant even from a philological point of view.

"Dóbroje útro!"[89] while, amazed, I held my hand in the clothes-bushes, tucked away in the corner of the cupboard: had they really imagined that I was going to take one of those Litevkas with me? (Mind you: why not, actually? Could show that off at home! ? Sure: just keep on stuffing that rucksack!). / And already nearly 9: I was oversleeping the never-to-be-repeated opportunity! — : "Is it raining heavily outside, Yelena?"

Yelena — she was willing alright. But I wasn't. I'd got up with that blasted feeling that nothing on earth, nor in the air, in fire or in water would please me today.

"Chotshesh li ty menya pravadits?; Meaning?" / 'Willya come along with me?' she said supposedly: what else was there finally left for me to do? / Downstairs, in front of the Gastinitsa, the other two were already waiting with their raincoats on: we greeted each other with undisguised grimness:!.

Here: Oh, Thou Grey Earth!: Considerate no more; it was morning; business was pressing.

The wolf hounds: "You were asking yesterday what happens to the brains of the young volunteers? — : Paszóltye!"[90] — — :

The Siberian wolf hounds. They leaped up. They looked at you so clever, so human. / And so they were: if I asked one of them, "Pythagoras?" — he promptly scribbled in the sand with his nibbed paw: $a^2 + b^2 = c^2$! / "Some know Russian — *and* American!" — and he stared at me significantly: I had become an important man: the umbilical cord holding the 2 worlds together: Oh, had I but stayed in my grove! / : *So these were the thieves of Inglefield's secret papers!!* — (And was gripped by deep compassion for the manager's huge wolfhound, who had pressed himself against my stroking hand. We (i.e., the West) are lost! ('Unless the Centaurs save us' — something whis-

---

[89] Good morning.
[90] Please.

pered way down in one of my sub-craters.) / Wasn't Uspenski raising his hand? — What was he saying?: "Wait a moment." —

A paddock: 2 horses grazing there. And his mouth folded into a more official shape. In the watchmaker's rain shop. / 1 mare: 1 stallion: Hengist & Horsa. / He grabbed my forearm. He commanded sternly: "Call out. — No: shall we say = uh: first 'Dshain'; then 'Steffan': Call out."

I crossed my arms over my chest (in order to have something to hold on to: everything slowly started spinning round!). — He looked at me stonefaced.: "Yelena?!" she looked at me, indifferent, interpreteusing, big titted. (All of a sudden I felt the vibration of the island again.) / But: if you are cold, so am I. (Let's give it a try) — :

"JANE! : STEPHEN!": They jerked their horse-heads aloft:?:!: Came up: first walked, then trotted, then at a gallop (then ventre à terre — how should I know what they call the racing end-spurt?!) —

Then quivering at the fence; and trembling. / And allowed themselves to be stroked. And hoof-scraping. (And that fat mare-stomach! Which Uspenski confirmed "Steffan has covered Dshain." Countless times. She bashfully turned her head aside, and emitted a spiritus asper. / And upon renewed stroking and whispering: they snorted in exasperation (must also have been inhibited by their ridiculously thick gonads: half horse, half human: horse latitudes!). —

Led away; I; the two brain-snatchers ahead of me. (Have abducted from us, the Free West, 2 master=minds: Oh, you villains!! / But Uspenski, very heavily):

"Tell your Mister Inglefield: We *would* have something to swap! — For — " (and now with awsome gravity): "we *too* are missing our two top chess players: World Champions Ryleyev; and Voveyko."

"We shall keep the brains in storage: until October 1: Tell that to Mister Inglefield!". / And I, though immune as an envoy (apart from which mine would hardly have been worth snitching!) decided once again to keep close to the wooden fence: Apuleius of Madaura was *not* joking! Make me strange stuff[91] If I should refuse... / They escorted me along their part of Harbour Street. The steady drizzle massage-rollered my brain.

But — *(I must be a born reporter after all;* for questions kept coming out: *some* questions?!): "So what will the end-product be?" (re the horses; Gregson and that Cappelman filly, assaulted by glands... — He shrugged his shoulders: "Centaurs maybe. — Comrade Shukovski?". But he didn't know either, "Wait and see": "Okay".

"Does the wolfhound recognize 'its body' again?": I mean, does the brain transplanted into the dog recognize its newly-brained, wandering body? — They furrowed their broad brows uneasily: "There *appears* to be a — uh=connection — not altogether crystal-clear as yet. The two often like to be together." (The dog tended to sleep in its master's chamber; whimpered when he was left behind. — But there were also instances when he bit him — that area hadn't been fully explored yet.)

The 'Zone-border': on the dripping wall the red poster howled: 'You are now leaving the Peace Camp!'. / Turn round once more. With an effort I asked — it was all just too much for one man — : "Mister Uspenski?: Who are you actually?!" / He bowed, the black bowler peacefully in his hand: "Head of the United Eastern Counter-Intelligence." And then, officially via Yelena: "I shall expect Mr. Inglefield at 11 o'clock in the Neutral Strip: Let's negotiate!" (A ceremonial "Dasvidânya"! All around.: "Goodbye, Sir").

---

[91] The author's version of Caliban's speech, *The Tempest,* Act IV. Tr.

Left standing between 2 wet high-rises (in front of the Town Hall): why isn't anybody collecting me? (Oh yes, of course; we hadn't agreed upon a specific time. / So I circumvoluted the pencilline tower (how long is a new pencil? Let's hold one against it.)[92] Past the archives (where an Indian, gloomy and beturbanned, deciphered a tome by the open window: strict customs they have there). / Then up the starboard side of Harbour Street, towards the hotel (and keep it nice and slow: collect thoughts. — No, man!: run! :they want to get out of that horse box again!!) —

Puffing, tears of rain still blubbering down my cheeks; puzzled, the janitor stood by me. / Until I could point: over there!: "Mister Inglefield.". / Sink into the chair meanwhile. (And leap up again right away: so, theoretically, one could sit down nowadays in a chair which was covered in one's own original skin! Be holding a book bound in one's own hide; with one's own warmly-lined 'personal'-leather-waistcoat round one's chest: I-nappa, you-nappa. Could slurp vodka from one's own skull-cup: pass it over, Rosamunda! Contemplate one's very own death's head, giggling! reverently behold your good ole self as a genuine skeleton in your study. — : One *could*.....
/Certainly: no problem!: If a strapping thirty-year old had her brain transplanted into a young man she could spend one or two nights with her own other-brained body. A chance finally to examine and inspect oneself critically: Pythagoras was nowhere by comparison — for he was never, after all, a man of simultaneity, but had been a linear man!). / — "Yes?: Yes, let me have it!!". — —

:"*Mister Inglefield?* — : *Can you come on over here imm=ee-diately?* / Oh, you've been waiting already? / Yes, quickly: Life & Death is the understatement of the year!"

---

[92] Everyone knows a new pencil is 7 inches long; so a rule is hardly called for, in fact.

And staring again at the wall-splendour: We Westerners really are *better!* / Now what species of human rape was this again!: Send us back the body; after all, they've got the crucial part! Preserve it in large animals; hide it in horses: what would Uspenski & Co do if no agreement was reached by October? — Throwitaway? Destroy it? (After Gregson had had to mount a whole bunch of Tartar=breeding=stud for them — which he might even have enjoyed getting stuck into; I should have asked). (Or out of spite transplant it into a shark with a horrendous surfeit of teeth?: "For a Soviet man nothing is eempossible."). / And now *this* cold calculation (definitely the last!) — let's take one of these clever wolfhounds: does he really feel so much more unhappy than when he was a human? There are types, — leather-stockinged from tip to toe, who even as humans voluntarily isolate themselves: who restlessly stomp around the forests in all kinds of weather: run wild and feed like wolves; their bed a lair of friendly foliage, old and pale, with the moon for their lamp and their hat for a roof. Into the bushes from time to time with something Indian, red-skinned and leathery!: wouldn't it be quite possible that one of those characters would blissfully and freely transform himself physically into one hell of a wolfhound? Then he could roam 200 kilometres a day with ease, instead of 60! And an elegant she-wolf of silver-grey pelt with every hair black-tipped, is no doubt considered preferable to Madame de Milo in vulpine circles. / (All sorts of witty tricks there: how that Tyras in question must have died of laughter when he took those secret papers off Inglefield. Or that one yesterday, who immediately introduced that expression about 'swapping' to Uspenski! Nope; most people — at least considering the current prevalent level of intelligence — couldn't care a fuck whether they ran around as wolves or talking humans.) / ..... / : If only Ing . . . :

"Ah, Mister Inglefield!" and I was just brimming over; but he stopped me by means of the tall black gentleman: "General

Coffin: our Zone Commander." / I stared at this new creature. I asked (bereft of reason anyway; for at least 3 days): "I thought — : professional soldiers aren't allowed to enter the Island?!": "General Coffin is *not* a professional soldier: each of our ordinary recruits has a marshall's baton in his knapsack." / (But that was just another of those damned Western strategies designed to outflank the enemy! Even if the Island charter did unfortunately only contain the word 'professional soldiers', it obviously and inarguably *meant* that 'martial spirit' as such just wasn't welcome here! Were we *again* the first to start up with such confounded tricks? — : "Who, as a matter of interest, is the Zone Commander over there?": "A certain Oklovski — a pianist", Inglefield answered coolly (and I gnashed to my innards: so it *was* us again who started to squabble!)).

"No; please: not till we're in the car!" (in the sound-proof, armoured, earthquake-resistant, ray-repellent what-have-you). / And report. / They listened. Asked. (Battle-conduct brief; I automatically answered back likewise in the old army style; till I gradually got a grip on myself, and pulled them up short.). / "Mister Inglefield?: write this down!" (And small, round, hard rules came tumbling out: all large dogs — "large animals in general" — to be tested, or rather exterminated. Warning the entire Free Island World.: "Hang on! This will have to be done first: Inglefield?!": / And was sworn in on a very black book which no one believed in any more; and had to sign a booklet without being allowed to read it even nominally, nor to discuss beforehand — "You've got the picture, Mister Winer?!" (As a matter of fact, *not quite;* but what could I do? : After all, I'd been sworn in a good dozen times already — i.e. 11 times too many (if not 12 times!); sworn not to breathe a word. (And had finally, at the very back of my brain, reserved a tiny compartment, into which I put all my oaths — so stuff this new one in there too, will have to fit in somehow; and put a lid on!). / And you lot, before you call me 'frivolous', or

something with 'un....' — like 'un-patriotic, =ethical, =principled' — : you'd do better to beat your oath-inventors'-breasts, and hard too, till you perish! Compared to yours, my hands are still lilly-white: may Uspenski take you!)))).[93]

And now things were to continue briskly: "So: at 11 o'clock Island-time, this uh=gentleman said?" (While the sound-proof vehicle flitted along with us grave-wards: not just in the stupid figurative sense of 'livingacontinualdying', 'walkingacontinualfalling'; but he'd actually called out to the (mechanical?) chauffeur: "The grave. Quick."). And why not, after all. Sooner or later one's number's gonna come up. At least I had lived it up a little. And created quite enough trouble for one lifetime. (Especially in this here flea-circus! How had Bob Singleton put it?: "If you stretched a tent across, you'd have the biggest circus in the world!" — I was beginning to be of this opinion myself!).

Standing next to the car (on whose Kreuder-green roof the rain babbled as if counting its change : 2 detached houses behind us; half a dozen of the same in front. We strode between them: towards the grave.)

"Of course 'Grave' is only just our internal shorthand for it — some refer to it as 'the Cannery': — the correct expression, as employed in official correspondence, would be 'Hibernation Research Institute'." / While we ambled through the sod =sputtered parklands that surrounded it. ('Hibernia'?: that was the ancient name for Ireland, if I knew my Ptolemy: was anyone who entered here swiftly changed into an Irishman?

---

[93] Incredible! Where is the point of an oath as such, given an attitude like the author's? The sacred covenant by the Witness of Heaven has proved its worth perfectly well in every war, as any recruit-training officer will tell you. Quite apart from the multifarious usefulness of civil oaths — although the oath-worthiness of each and every subject to be sworn in should be unimpeachable in every case! / I won't bother to mince words about the revolting picture of four brackets following hard upon each other's heels.

Squat redhaired lying fairytale-tongued inebriate graveling? (Ohyes, pugnacious as well, right).). / Howling gusty gales tumbled across the forest; and we came up to the main entrance: the slinky black tom-cat nestling around the post had been woefully scolding the weather, and asked to be let in with us: but Inglefield bawled back, "No!". — On second thoughts he grabbed the astonished creature in a formidable hold: "Name?!" (cutting; inquisitional; he wouldn't let go until, after a hair-raising pause it confessed: "Miaou." — And the two military buffs nodded more grimly at one another: aha — so: a disguised Chinaman: Mao! "Keep your eye on him, Inglefield!").

In an entrance hall: Grave paintings on the walls. (Mostly resurrection scenes: pious Yankees floating upwards between skyscrapers, with little star-spangled banners between their supplicating hands). In the centre of the hall a female angel of silence attired in a tight-fitting chemist's smock: earnestly she glanced at me, her gloved finger impressive=vertical raised to her charmingly=officious pair of lips. (Plus a hefty whiff of antiseptic.)

"Inglefield?: 10:50: You'd better set out for the check point. — You're adequately acquainted with the conditions. — No, I'll stay here; can be contacted any time." / So he made himself scarce. While we stepped into a 'right' conference-room (where 2 white-smocks were already awaiting us (and a goddess in nurse's uniform: overpoweringly pale from innumerable all-night vigils (some might even have been at sickbeds); nun-like sacrifice, alabasterized, immaculate, 'I must remain a virgin, until the chief-surgeon takes me.' / For a single brief instant her eyes let loose a lascivious skyblue flash.)

The briefing. / *While she enfolded* me in sweet snowy shackles, literally: helped me into a smock (just like yesterday!); crowned me with a white beret. Thou shalt be the Master of my Soul. Then the sterilized=stinking pad over my mouth. And finally the net of the muslin bandage; in which she caught and swathed me: round and round. / Then another vaccination: she pulled back the white linen foreskin of my wrist, teased cunningly with the ether-wad — and shoved the needle in (Oh topsy-turvy world). Gazed absent=present into mine eyes whilst she squirted her contents into me. / And from behind the attendant doctor was explaining: that it derived rather from 'hibernus':

"We"; had already discovered early on, that the life-functions could be slowed down by cold — "death from exposure." With appropriate refrigeration the heart only beats once every minute: organic wear and tear was practically eliminated! "After many and multiple" — (The fine distinctions they were hip to!) — "experiments in this direction, we had progressed so far by 1980 that we could guarantee a safe twenty-year long hibernation — during which time the organism in question ages by about 15 weeks." / (So if that one lay down at 60 in 1980: and woke up in the year 2000 — he'd still be only 60 years old! Lived for another 5 years, and presumably had himself a ball: lay down again: continued snoozing...?)

"In here, please": first a two-inch door-sized pane of glass; an assistant was removing the putty-strip with a bronze blade: "We are in the process of inducing an 'awakening'; you shall be a personal witness." / And — while 2 other men let the glass-board tilt towards them and disappeared with it — I remembered all sorts of puzzling things from yesterday which were beginning to fall into place: so that hermit, the old dog, was only 60 then, in fact, and had merely lain 'in the grave'? *That's* why Inglefield, when I, the little innocent, had said that he'd wake up again some time.....: aha! (Without being any happier for all my new-found knowledge! Just then the steel door came ajar).

Another glass-plate! — But *this* time it was transparent. / The assistant stuck in his knife-tip again; the doctor continued speaking:

"*We are planning* — long term, you might of course object" — (Me?: I couldn't object to a dickybird with the muslin-gag on my jaw! And yet I did have questions . . .) — : "to periodically sink the whole of humanity into hibernation: so that, in the not too distant future, one will be able to differentiate between a 'waking generation' and a 'sleeping generation'. A small group of the waking keeps an eye on the sleepers, housed in hundred-storey towerblocks. Life-span of 3 to 400 years will become the norm; quite apart from the fact that — with the corresponding further development of the 'storing' method — the Free World will have room for twice the population." / My white ghost staggered in between 4 comparable ones (not similar, please!) — into this Newest Holy of Holies: there were beginning to be too many for me! —

Step up to the glass-bell: — . — . — . : Ohsatan! (Eyes shut: keep your eyes shut!: This was even worse than Jane's pregnant mare!). / The air stank: disinfected. —

Those hair mountains!!!: They'd grown through the pillow at the back; metre-long clanging nails on fingershapes. / And he explained — one can even get used to hell: didn't some German say that, 'I'll bet'? Did after all produce some great men.[94] Even without hibernation.

Feeding drips tipped in, through tubes, the liquid spurted into the stomach once a week: then gentle rubber-bubbles immediately sucked at the bottom of them, to evacuate faeces poison, and the bladder. Black and poisonous (and smelly), the faeces were being yanked out of her body by the assistant,

---

[94] At last! (Grabbe, 'Gothland') — Although the author, when confronted with this, once again tried to talk himself out of it with *the usual:* only in Germany would one have had cause to hit upon such maxims.

heave-ho. And coiffed her a page-boy atop. In a sudden access of insane humour, I asked for one of the nails: *and graciously received it; souvenir, oh souvenirs!!*).

Stiff joints. Atrophy of the muscles: the foot-soles had gotten thin as paper (sensitive; compulsory exercise). The punctures pricked over a twenty-year period healed up very slowly : stick a beauty-patch over it, eh?! / Clocks buzzing meanwhile on every wall. / Now turn to the master poet (whose name I'd never again be able to read without shuddering: I was paying dearly for my Island trip!): and with him too the nails had fallen over one another like the bones of a giant fish. He also lay in skeletal confinement, and fasted towards his waste.

And now the awakening: ? — : He himself, lui-même, el mismo, took a syringe of fearsome proportions in his hand. Filled with crystalclear stuff: nowadays could be whisky, digitalis, glass-coffin, belladonna: Just keep on fixin'!! — Applied it — : and stabbed deep: deep!: into the skeleton-girl: Twentyone, twentytwo: twentythree: what do I know; I'm just a poor ole nigger Winer from Douglas on the Kalamazoo! . . . .

(And waiting: the Doc, the General, me; and the white hot piece. Among human tin-cans. In the grave. And all the clocks ticking over . . . .):

And waiting . . . . . / *It had started* to get noisy outside. Whole lotta fighting goin' on: voice against voice; reason against cause: the cause won:! / The General wrinkled his brow (while studying the note he held in his untrembling hand: mine would have wobbled. But they must've been used to these page-boy numbers.) — "Tell Inglefield: we'd offer that too!" (And then whispered about the 'that'. I turned away; none of my business!).

And waiting: the doctor was now wrinkling his smooth forehead . . . . / "Ahhh!"

Draw back the curtain-fringe of your lashes!: the tall girl obviously didn't see a thing. (How that page-boy fringe striated her brow! — Shut again; she didn't want to yet (i.e., to live).) The clocks clickety=clicking away. / And the master-poet obviously not playing: I was highly amused by the way he refused to unlatch his eye! (They injected, and grumbled into the tulle=net.)

In the corridor: on one of the doors it said, in beautifully curlicued characters, 'R&V' (below that, tastefully, the Hammer & Sickle emblem and 1 chessboard). I looked at my escorts: ?. And they confirmed with a brief nod: "Ryleyev and Voveyko." ('For swapping').

Bandage off my mouth; notebook in my hand (here's something good you can hold on to! Especially in a well-furnished room. And let them describe the details of the 'awakening'):

First the piercing pain at the side (— in the wrists, in fact — from the wake-up=jab.) / Very slowly to begin with; very slowly a thumb moved 'below' when 'I' gave the command, 'above'. / Warped semi-consciousness — : "But they sleep in shorter and shorter shifts: 6 days for a kick-off; 5, 4, 3; then 2 for a while; finally 1 night: normal." / "Excrement like pitch and tar, I admit: feeding is actually the most difficult problem for the first month." / Luxuriate in orgies of 'Living=Angst'?: "That happens. Is the rule, in fact; for men as well as women." (As soon as a partner emerges from the bas-relief of first impressions; that's how they establish relations again most quickly and effectively.)

They had set out all sorts of things here, in the 'well-furnished room', for the resurrected: a large illustrated magazine covering the years slept away — technology, fine arts, literature: X had become a great man; Y'd died of booze — the 'Memory-Crash' — they had technical terms for everything! — not everybody's cup of tea. / "Who writes the textbooks for the dormice?" : A Committee. (Of course, who else). "It's not all that easy!" (they; with emphasis; because I showed too little surprise for their liking: but I didn't have much left to show!).

(*And the poet had dried up*, the old coward!!: I could have jumped up, dance=beating my fists together (and warbled the Bergamasque-Dance from 'Tiefland' in obligato): serves him right! After all he had completely lost touch with the rest of humanity such as us! He slept and enjoyed whatever he could: we burned ourselves up — while he lived 'forever'.: Well, that'll teach you! / "But this is in fact only the eighth time that we.....".)

A new Courier?: General Coffin jutted out his jaw. *Far* out! What's more, crossed his arms over his chest. Weighed responsibilities against each other (but what if his counter was out?!); slowly moved his hand to his breast-pocket (slowly; that was something anyway; at least it looked as if he was thinking about it — although I knew from my army days that that's not general practise with them). / Slowly he pulled out the top-secret notebook. He began and printed in block letters:.......!.......:!! ....:!!! — / And – after a final iron-hard pause — his name at the bottom: COFFIN! / (Had the negotiations fallen through? Or was he signing the contract? Was it a final offer? Or had Inglefield perhaps abducted Uspenski? Or rather had that one transformed him into a polarhound? Or had they both put each other to sleep: for 20 years!?).

Then the final smart-alecky question: "What if during these 20 somno=years something=uh happens?" (War, of course. 'Andthelike'? — Understood me at once; although he acted dumb):

"*It is not our task*, to take that into consideration." And further: "One mustn't even think of that." (And I nodded, smiling politely: if you'd given a different answer, that'd make you a Phoenix, sure thing! Or a suicide-case. — I wouldn't have

Coffin's kisser for any money: not even for Fort Knox! (Or wait: for that, sure; then nothing would matter!).). / The nun announced that the roused poetess had just taken three deep breaths: so everything had worked out alright (and the doctors rushed out. In case she should breathe again.)

(*Another quarter of an hour* leafing through the textbooks, and flirting with Lady White: only once before had I come across someone as depraved as that! She used expressions (always under the guise of medical precision) which could blow your mind on the spot! Her kiss tasted like a squirt of Lysol laced with penicillin — but by then I didn't have a care in the world!).

Outside, past the Otsego=Lake: "*Abdallá!: Abdallá!:*" the island crows were shouting for my return-journey: the human form had become a joke for me! (I'd rather have a clump of shrubs than Stupin's bush! — In future I'm gonna camouflage my bones in plant=shapes and =colours, so's I have to think less of myself. / Was feeling quite dizzy. As if on a turntable.)

Turntable?: Even my General placed his legs more like an old seadog. We swayed our torsos in front of each other: I didn't feel at all well! (Probably just me noticing the shakes — : enough to make *any*one lose his appetite!). —

God!: was that actually happening? Or not?: Makes you feel right queasy in the tum!: ?! / Coffin belched. Coffin pinched his mouth. He said: "This Mr=uh Uspenski: didn't go along with our conditions. I've therefore given the appropriate order to our machine-sector: to let the propellors run full speed *aback*: we must return to USAmerican territorial waters! Get the hell out of these insane Doldrums: then we'll show those Bolshies!" / And taken back in zig-zag lines by the (mechanical?) chauffeur. / "No: keep going. To the TV-studio."

(1300 Hours: it was about time for me to figure out what I was going to enter into the Golden Book in the way of a goodbye! Hoped I'd conjure up some sort of non-commital razmataz. / And, while the compact car waltzed over the asphalt with us burpers, I was getting on with memorizing some key-words: 'granted; surprise; unforgettable hours: looked after; farewell; lovely time.' (Or rather, no: the 'lovely time' nearer the beginning, the 'farewell' at the end: should I bring in 'port=and=starboard' as well? — My, if I could just keep all that together!).).

No, he was not mechanical after all: the chauffeur! He steered us with pronounced meandering through the Neutral Strip and belched with the best: are we all sloshed then?! (Mind you: in my case it could be the fix that pale-faced sperm-sucker had rammed into my veins; who knows what that contained.) / What sort of a meeting was taking place?: The Island Committee? Because of little insignificant *me*?! —

Yes!! (And be festive now, Winer! : this act was being broadcast the whole world over, via the moon! — Or rather, to that *half* of the globe; for which it stood over the horizon!)

:*"Mister Winer!"* : all on wavelength 17.892. I tried to shape my mug into a more enthusiastic expression; for up front the white-haired Indian of yester-year was talking away; and an usher mumbled into my ear: that it was all for *my* sake! ("Mine? Winer's?": "Yes, you!: Shhh!").

And was, in solemn plenary session, appointed 'Hon Doctor, IRAS'!: Me: Charleshenry!![95] (My God, in that case I'd have to alter my Goldenbookentry again! Our hands, those bestowing a certificate and those accepting one, were trembling; our

---

[95] Depressing, the recklessness with which academic honours can be distributed. A man with a sense of responsibility would have turned it down in a case like this: Domine, non sum dignus! That sort of modest self-knowledge is, however, utterly foreign to Mr — I mean Dr! — Winer!

faces presumably still solemn; but also chalk-white, both of them; both swallowed: "Please: hic.": "Hic=thanks!").

And in procession, in cap and gown, back to the Town Hall again: ghastly cheerfulness, sardonic on every escort=face; it just couldn't all be in order! / (And the mouth of the old Indian whispered at one of my ears — I couldn't tell which one any more —: "The Americans have ordered 'Full Speed Reverse'; the Russians 'No change — Full Speed Ahead'." / "And the result?").

The result?: "We are rotating!: On the same spot!" /The outer edges of the Island had by now got up a speed of 5 metres per second (which would go up to 10 once everything had been co-ordinated! When it was to complete a full revolution in 25 minutes. At 150° longitude and 38 latitude: in the middle of the Pacific Sargasso Sea, in the calm regions, the Doldrums...). : "Does my plane happen to be ready?"

"Oh come now: the Golden Book first!" (Can one live on a turntable? Make love? And if so: then to what effect? The usual? or does one keep slipping off? / 'The moon revolves': some long time ago a dumb poet had babbled that blather, and then it was just a completely cocked-up metaphor: now we've got it! Now it revolved! / I stamped my foot.)

Held up by an Arab on my right, and a Lotus-type on my left; up the steps to the Town Hall: they would not let me go, except I signed! (What were all those words? Farewelllooked-afterbeautifulandgranted — Oh my — just so long as I don't go and puke all over their fine book! . . . .)

A hall, a=hall: hadn't I been here before? / I fell onto the chair — for which brief relief much thanks; but not for long: quite the contrary! Exercise & fresh air! — and gaped emptily into the turmoil: how crooked that desk was here! I laughed idiotically at some speaker-type: yeah, you aren't feeling all that kosher either! / Groped around for the antique pen — and the lines on the beautiful paper slowly began to serpentangle themselves before my eyes, Ohspiralofmine. I swallowed hard to get that Russian breakfast down again: 'Surprisegranted-unforgettableandhours'. / They obviously wanted to have done with it, too. I took aim at the paper; gripped at the table's edge with my unemployed left hand. And wrote (my jaws full of caviar again!): What?:

'*I grant* the Island management a surprising farewell. / Rarely have I been so relieved by beauties, never so tended by portsiders: each rotation will remain unforgettable for me!' / (And hastily add my signature thereto:!).

On the street to the airport: they were obviously in a hurry to get me out of the way. (And so was I: nuttin but home by jet! Brr!). / Still negotiating. The Indians meanwhile tried to stop the rotation with Yoga — they might just as well have tried with yoghurt!: "Your great-great-uncle never thought of anything like this, what?" (The rotation?: "No; I'm sure he didn't!").

Airfield; 2 trees, sighing at each other: the rain stoning us with glass-sweets. —

Island farewell: a tiny yellow hand in mine. / Before I threw up: "What do you think, Pandit Dshaganath: what will happen?" / He slowly lifted his shoulders.: "Whichever machines happen to last out longer; port or starboard. — Maybe it will even rip straight down the middle: the long-term effect of those sort of push and pulling powers were not taken into account when it was built — according to the engineers ....." (and again the affecting shoulder-movement). —

Vertically it stood, and spread its powerfully jet-propelled fists: get in!!! — — . — : !! — — — : !!! — — — — : !! — — — — — — !!!! !!!! !!!!

★   ★
★

"Well, pilot?" : and he too moved his head in bewilderment: most odd! / (And yet I was tickled when he called me 'Doc': Vanity, Thy name is Winer!). —

Propel higher over the rolling Island: quite nice and peaceful it looked from up here. / "Oh, 5.000 kilometres to Detroit! : we'll be there in 3 hours!" / (So that made it roughly 1900 hours. Then to Great Rapids with the next machine: 2000 in all. Or 21 at the most. Ring up Frederick from there: he'll pick me up in the car: Groovy. I moved my shoulders in the safety belts.)

But that pilot was an educated man!: 'Once I lived like the Gods, and I need nothing more' he quoted laughing (and envious of me: that I'd been allowed to see 'All That'. / "Ohwell," I said evasively, and gave out a few unimportant details: you can jolly well read my articles!). —

(What was then the most decisive image out of these mad days? / — (First of all relax totally. Cross out everything. Switch back completely to 'before': what *had* made the strongest impression on me? / I knew myself: I just had to wait and see; then a very bright flash, a snap-shot, from my picture-reservoire . . . . .) . . . .) : There!:

The curtains began to flutter: parted: to the right, to the left . . . . . : A horse-women crossing the sand-plain! Passed me without stopping: only turned her face, and looked me straight in the eyes through an oversized golden = corn-ear:!:

"Thalia!!" / (Passed me without halting: not the Indian, not the Russian, not the nurse and not the lanky sculptress. (Even Queen Shub-ad rather than that.)) / Thalia.

I slammed my hand down on my safety-strapped knee: but tomorrow morning straight into the reed-isle of the Kalmazoo in my very own canoe! — . —

(And again, what an idea?: 'Once I had lived like the Gods'!!!). —